Seeds of
Destruction

Seeds of Destruction

A. V. Denham

ROBERT HALE · LONDON

ISBN 0 7090 7901 X

Robert Hale Limited
Clerkenwell House
Clerkenwell Green
London EC1R 0HT

2 4 6 8 10 9 7 5 3 1

Typeset in 11/15pt New Century Schoolbook
by Derek Doyle & Associates, Shaw Heath.
Printed in Great Britain by St Edmundsbury Press
Bury St Edmunds, Suffolk.
Bound by Woolnough Bookbinding Ltd.

Acknowledgements

The characters bear no resemblance to any persons, living or dead.

Thanks to Jackie Neale from *Gyrfa Cymru Career Wales* for helpful advice on mature students and the teaching profession. Also to Breast Cancer Care who publish a useful series of pamphlets on the disease (also available in Welsh). Any errors in the interpretation of their advice are mine. *Anglo-Welsh*, of whose boats we have fond memories, operate out of Great Haywood and other canal boatyards.

My thanks especially go to the editorial team at Robert Hale yet again for invaluable editorial advice.

Chapter One

Amanda

The rippling chords of the second movement of the Rachmaninov concerto came to their spine-tingling end. The radio DJ said: 'That dedication was, *And for my other family. . . .*'

Amanda Williams, standing spellbound at the old and battered scrubbed-pine kitchen table with a knife motionless in her hand, resumed slicing onions for dinner. She sniffed, and the tears began to fall, though whether from the onions or the music she didn't know. She reached for a tissue and blew her nose violently. The dedication was intriguing. *And for my other family. . . .* A second marriage, all the heartbreak that followed the collapse of a first relationship, the relief when it was all over?

Amanda shook her head. She was not going down that path now. She had far too much to do. Mentally she ticked off the jobs: clean sheets, lager in the fridge, wine for Sunday, enough food in the house to feed an army (a growing son and a husband, not to mention her brother and his wife). She smiled with satisfaction for an hour well spent since school as she heard the front door open.

'I'm in the kitchen, love. Got wet hands,' she called.

Almost immediately he was there, behind her, his arms round her, nuzzling her neck.

'Mmm, missed you,' he growled, as his hug threatened to crack her ribs. 'Did you miss me?'

She turned in his arms smiling up at him.

'What do you think?' There was a long moment of mutually beneficial reunion. When they both paused to draw breath, Joe Williams indicated a large bunch of flowers he had thrown on to a kitchen chair.

'Gorgeous. Sweet-williams have always been one of my favourites, and they're particularly good this year.' She admired the intense colours, deep pink, a purple that was almost black. 'Are they from her garden?'

'Picked them myself. Never was able to make a proper bouquet, though.'

'As if that matters.'

'And there's a treacle tart for you this week. She made it yesterday.'

'There's kind of her. Simon and his friends cleaned me out last night and I haven't had time to do any baking since.'

She dried her hands and went over to the fridge, opened the door and took out two cans of lager. Then she followed her husband as he left the kitchen. He pulled off his tie and threw it on to the hall table before he went into the sitting-room.

'Have you had a good week?' she asked as she handed him a can.

'Not bad,' he answered, sitting back on the battered tweed-covered sofa, relic of the days when Simon and his best friend were always climbing over the furniture whatever you said to them about the garden being a more suitable place for games of chase. Joe gulped half the lager appreciatively. 'How about you, everything all right?'

She snapped open a can of lager for herself, her thick, dark hair which she wore cut straight just below her shoulders, falling in rippling waves round her face and concealing her appreciation at the predictability of their encounter so far.

'Fine, dear, fine,' she answered vaguely, wondering whether to tell him about . . . But he caught her free hand in his and pulled her down beside him. 'There's another where that came from, when you're ready. She smiled fondly at him as she reflected that it wouldn't have done any good and how different he was from Michael. . . . The lager went down the wrong way and she choked. That was the second time Michael had come into her mind. She'd not thought of him for so long.

Joe was her husband. He was also the most handsome man she knew, with his brown wavy hair, not a hint of grey in it yet, strong tanned features, a smile that would melt the stoniest-hearted, dark-brown eyes with their warm and intense gaze that took her back to the earliest days of their courting, and which still set her heart to fluttering. Having Joe at home only at the weekends was like a perpetual honeymoon.

'How's Si?'

'Good. He's got a home match on Saturday.'

'Excellent. Haven't seen him play for ages. I'll wander down and spend the afternoon watching him.'

'He'd like that,' Amanda answered warmly. 'He was talking about it only yesterday.' It was a bit difficult, with Joe away most of the week, though she knew he generally went to watch his son, if he had the time. But you couldn't have everything, and generally she-they managed, from Monday to Thursday.

She got up and sighed inwardly as she went into the kitchen where she threw the empty cans into the bin with an unnecessary clatter. It wasn't fair of her to complain, even to herself. Joe worked hard, had always worked hard at the business, to provide for herself and their son.

Joe had drifted into the kitchen in time to hear the bang of the waste-bin as she shut it.

'You upset about something?' he asked, sounding concerned.

Amanda straightened her back and took a deep breath

before she replied calmly:

'No, dear. Whatever gave you that idea?'

'The noise,' he told her succinctly.

'The can slipped out of my hand.'

'That's all right, then.' Joe put his arm round Amanda's shoulders and gave her a quick hug. She relaxed almost immediately. 'That's better, love. I'm going to take my shower now. Be down shortly. That all right with you?' And when she nodded, her soft mouth once again upturned in a smile, he gave her bottom a loving stroke before going upstairs.

Joe owned a firm which made agricultural machinery and, because he was an ambitious man who enjoyed the cut and thrust of competition – and from a sense of family pride, he also managed his aunt's works. Joe and Amanda had met at a club in Croydon nineteen years before and he had swept her off her feet at that first meeting and later she had actually allowed him to set aside all her doubts (along with her knickers) that same evening on the back seat of his car.

Afterwards she had cried, at home in her bed-sit, alone in bed. She couldn't understand herself – she'd only had two Bacardi and cokes, and hadn't she been through enough to make her vow never to let another man touch her again? For Amanda had been married before.

She had been persuaded to go to that club by a friend at the supermarket who had suggested a night out.

'Oh, I'm not sure . . .'

'What's the problem; you're divorced aren't you?'

'Not exactly . . .'

'Bastard, was he?'

Amanda told her an expurgated version of the sorry tale.

'Good thing you ditched the git. Now go and enjoy yourself,' said the girl friend, robustly supportive.

At the time the advice had seemed good. It was different

once Amanda realized she was pregnant. Even then, becoming a single mother had more than its fair share of social problems. There was the financial side, too, for she could barely support herself on her wages at the supermarket. Amanda had thought long into several nights. Her new GP, not knowing about the failed marriage, assumed the baby was her husband's and she never brought up the subject of abortion – it was not one that was brought up automatically in those days. Adoption scared her. Then, astonishingly, she discovered she wanted the baby, wanted someone she could love unstintingly without the fear of that love being unreciprocated. Wanted Joe's baby?

Something in Amanda's brain clicked and resettled itself. Unlikely as it seemed, she had fallen in love with this man who had made her pregnant. How long had they known each other? Reason said: not long enough, but reason didn't come into it. Joe had crept under her skin and into her heart and reason would dislodge neither him nor his baby.

Her family would undoubtedly want to compare Joe with Michael. They would say she could not possibly know her own mind — had she not already proved that? But it wasn't true. This time she was sure; of Joe and that she loved him.

The only question was just how much Joe loved her.

Bravely she told him about the baby, and waited humbly for — truly she knew not what. If he refused to have anything to do with her, with them, it would break her heart but it would make the baby all the more hers. What happened was not what she'd expected.

'Wow, a baby?' Joe was over the moon. 'It's a bit of a shock, but cripes, that's marvellous.' He declared at once that he'd stand by her. 'But the only thing is, even if we could, with Michael refusing a divorce and all that, I don't think I am the marrying kind.'

At first Amanda did not think she'd heard him right. He'd

stand by her surely meant marriage. She burst into tears. It took time for him to calm her down.

'But why should that make any difference?' he demanded, at last. 'What's to stop us from just setting up house together, bringing up the baby, becoming a family?'

'What happens if Michael changes his mind and gives me a divorce?' she had asked him.

'I just don't see the point of a civil marriage, of making vows to stay together for ever. Either we love each other and will stay together, or we won't. No ceremony is going to make any difference to our feelings. Look what happened to you and your husband. You thought you loved him once, didn't you?'

'Of course I did. He loved me, too.'

'But it didn't last. That's what I'm getting at. Don't you trust me?'

'You're not married already?' Amanda had whispered uncertainly.

'Me? Married already. What do you take me for? A total philanderer? I'm the one who's more likely to wonder about your past. Whether you . . . Ah, sorry. I shouldn't have said that.'

'No, you shouldn't. And do you mind if we don't talk about it? He–he wasn't a kind man. I'm just so thankful I left him when I did. There's another thing. I haven't yet told my parents. They don't even know about you, let alone the baby.'

'We'll tell them straight away.'

'I've got to do it alone,' she said firmly. 'They're a bit strait-laced. I'm not sure what their reaction will be. I'd rather you were not there.'

'If you insist,' Joe said.

She thought at the time that he sounded relieved. Well, and of course he was. She knew exactly what her parents' reaction would be. Shock. Horror, etc., etc. No man would want to face a critical older generation who would lay the blame of her pregnancy squarely on him. She gave up her job. She gave up the bed-sit she'd taken on to preserve her independence which was no hardship, it being small, dark and damp. She went home, telling Joe that she would call him as soon as possible.

Her parents had been on an extended winter holiday to Malta – it saved on their pensions – and had only just returned.

'I've met a wonderful man,' she told them, after they'd eaten and she'd seen their photographs. 'His name is Joe and he's kind and caring and everything Michael wasn't.'

Their initial reaction was one of caution.

'Isn't it a bit soon to start on another relationship?'

By relationship she knew that they meant friendship. She took a deep breath.

'I – we fell in love.'

Her father clicked his tongue in exasperation.

'Like it or not, you are still married to Michael. Has he agreed to divorce you yet? No,' he answered himself. 'This could jeopardize everything.'

'Joe had – has nothing to do with what happened with Michael. The thing is, we never meant it to happen but I'm pregnant.'

'Is he going to stand by you?'

They meant: is he going to marry you eventually? Amanda explained. There was a huge row in which shock, horror, etc. was hissed, shouted (her father) and wept over (her mother). In the end, though, the fact that there was to be a baby and that there would seem to be a husband persuaded Amanda's mother that they had better go along with it. 'Though what everyone will say doesn't bear thinking about.'

'They'll get over it,' Amanda maintained stoutly, 'neighbours and family.' She wondered just how true that was.

Mr and Mrs Wentwood were pillars of their parish community. They had been very much against her leaving Michael, let alone the idea of a divorce, even though they had never really cared for Michael. Yet they still said things like *making beds and lying on them*. This was even worse: that their daughter should subscribe to the new-fangled notion that living together without benefit of clergy (or the dubious blessing of the civil authorities) was acceptable. Selfish, her mother called him. Her father used more earthy language.

Maybe Joe was different, they conceded eventually, once the shock was over. They shook their heads, because he could have waited a little before making her pregnant, but a gleam of future grandmotherly anticipation shone in Mrs Wentwood's eyes. They could not wait to meet him.

'I've not told him very much about Michael. We've agreed not to mention him again. You do understand?'

'I always said you should never . . . Oh, well, water under the bridge,' agreed her father gruffly. 'I just hope this one—'

'Dad. . . .'

They met Joe and approved, after Joe assured Mr Wentwood that he could afford to keep their daughter in the manner to which they aspired. Then they set about parcelling Amanda off to South Wales, where Joe had decided to invest money that his mother had left him, in light engineering. Out of sight was out of mind, when all was said and done, the senior Wentwoods declared, and if they delayed telling the neighbours the exact date of the birth there would be no clacking of tongues.

So Joe and Amanda settled in what was then Gwent and Amanda took Joe's name – he said he didn't mind and it was one sop to her parents' pride. In due course Simon was born and it seemed to Amanda that everything she had ever wanted in her life was now hers. Michael had even agreed to divorce her for desertion. (She discovered through a mutual friend that he had met someone else.)

Joe adored his son. He would lean over the white-painted

wooden crib with its *broderie anglaise* frills which had been Amanda's when she was a baby with a yearning look on his face that made her stomach turn over with love for her family.

Then it happened. Joe received a letter from his Aunt Ethel, asking him to go and see her as she had business to discuss.

'It'll mean I'd have to stay overnight, I suppose. You'll be all right, will you?'

'I'm sure we will. Don't forget to give me a ring when you get there.'

The promised call came, but he stayed away for three days. When he came back her life changed irrevocably.

'I love you,' he said. 'I love Simon. But there's a problem.'

'What problem?' demanded Amanda, white-faced from exhaustion because Simon was teething. She knew she was still fat, ratty-haired and oozed milk when she wasn't actually breast-feeding.

'Aunt Ethel. You remember Aunt Ethel?'

'I suppose so. Wasn't she the one in the hat at the party my parents gave for us before we moved? She gave us the ghastly pottery soup-tureen. Despite all her money.'

'I think it's more valuable than we realize,' he said cautiously, but did not elaborate when he saw her stony face. 'Didn't I ever tell you about Aunt Ethel?'

'Probably,' said Amanda wearily, unsuccessfully trying to burp their son. 'Maybe you'd better remind me.'

Ethel Lansbury had been very good to Joe's mother when she was a child with TB. Now there was no one left, except Joe. Aunt Ethel was frail, he explained.

'She's convinced she's dying and she's decided to leave all her money to me,' he said.

'And that's a problem!' exclaimed Amanda. She had begun to quail inwardly at the prospect of nursing an elderly woman whom she'd met only once, as well as coping with a baby and

15

feeling mean and selfish at the same time. Simon burped and yawned and gently she put him into his cot.

'The money's mine, provided I take over her business. Light engineering. Not too different from what I do already. Her father started it and she carried on when he had a heart attack. Point is, there's scope to run the two businesses together. But it'd mean I'd have to be away Monday to Thursday. Keep an eye on her at the same time. If you agree.'

Amanda forgot about Aunt Ethel at the prospect of not having Joe at home. Appalled, she wept. Joe was adamant. She began to plead.

'Why can't you commute? How can I manage on my own?'

'It's too far. Look, I wouldn't think of suggesting it if I didn't know just how well you could manage.' The fingers of the hands which had given her nothing but pleasure kneaded away the tension in her clenched fists. 'Think of the advantages. What it will mean eventually to us and Simon. You can have help in the house. And Aunt Ethel is a sort of obligation, a debt of honour,' he pointed out in his turn.

'There are such things as homes,' said Amanda forthrightly.

'Not for Aunt Ethel, there aren't. She's far too proud.'

Scared rigid, then, that he might not even come home on Thursdays, Amanda agreed reluctantly. Alone with the baby, she berated herself for succumbing to emotional blackmail. Hadn't her parents warned her what would happen if Joe didn't marry her? But would a piece of paper make any difference, even now? He had promised he would only be away for part of the week.

It had been hell, at first. Bringing up a baby on her own was never going to be easy. Being solely responsible for Simon's welfare was exhausting all the time, nerve-racking when he was unwell. Sometimes Amanda wondered how she had managed, but the weekends had made it all worthwhile. Then, she still loved Joe and was convinced it was for the good of them all – and that it wouldn't last for ever. When he arrived home she only had to look at him for her insides to melt. Even now she melted, every Thursday, when he returned home for the weekend.

That had been the problem. There had been eighteen years of it, and Joe still managed both businesses. Times had been hard, but it had worked and they were not short of material things. There were good holidays. They ate out. He drove a BMW. There was a small car in the garage for her, changed every second year.

In other ways theirs was a good union. For all that he was away half the week, Joe was her rock, her support, her love. Smoothing her hands over her apron, Amanda set about feeding her son.

'Tea ready, Mum?' Simon erupted into the kitchen, five foot eleven, dark-hair fashionably shorn – a crime against nature, his mother thought – a hard-muscled young male with the looks of his father nineteen years ago and the long-lashed dark eyes that young women would kill for. She put a plate piled high with grilled steak, mushrooms, onion rings and chips, decorated with watercress in front of him.

'Oh, Mum. You know I don't like greens. And where are my best jeans?' he asked with his mouth full. As well as being an excellent cricketer, Simon played the drums for his school's jazz band. He was good at that, too, and had also formed a group which played for local events whenever local organizers could be persuaded to give them a gig.

'In the airing-cupboard. Didn't you look there first?' Amanda replied, ignoring the complaint about greenstuff. 'Eat it slowly. You'll get indigestion,' she warned Simon automatically. 'What are you doing this evening?'

'Revision. I've got a bit to get through and there'll be a dance after the match and I'm . . . a crowd of us're going to see the new Russell Crowe tomorrow evening.'

The crowd meant Lindy, she supposed, and the back row. It seemed to Amanda that being the mother of a son was as fraught with danger as being the mother of a daughter, which other mothers always argued was worse.

'As long as you take care.' The warning was out before she could prevent it.

'Care, Mum?' Simon gazed at her, wide-eyed and wholly innocent.

'You know very well what I mean,' she said indignantly, then she ran her palm over his bristly head. 'And get her home before eleven o'clock. I don't want an irate father round again. Where are you going now? I thought you were staying in,' as he reached for his house keys.

'Back soon but can't stop, Mum. Mick'll be here soon.'

'Where are you going with Mick?'

'Mick's father knows where we can get hold of some leather jeans cheap,' he explained, picking up an apple. 'It'll give us a new image, some decent gear.'

'Image.' She rolled her eyes. 'This revision you mentioned?'

'I'll do it when I get back.'

'I've heard that before. Oh, very well. Just you make sure the jeans haven't fallen off a lorry, and stick to the soft drinks. You hear!'

'Yes, Mum.' Simon gulped his tea and dashed out of the room. There was a pause. He shot back, kissed Amanda on the top of her head.

Amanda sat down weakly. Then she laughed. 'God help the girl you marry.'

'Marry, Mum?' Pausing in the doorway, Simon sounded shocked. 'Wouldn't think of committing such a folly. Not ever! Not for years. Not until the free supply runs short.'

'Get out,' she answered fondly. 'And stop trying to shock me,' as her son left the room grinning from ear to ear. A moment later the front door slammed.

'Seen anything of John this week?' Joe asked, entering the kitchen. He was freshly showered, his pale chinos and denim shirt showing off well-preserved early middle-age. 'I hope they're coming for Sunday lunch. I want his advice on an engine knock.'

John was Amanda's elder brother, who had recently married. He had kept very quiet about Fay. Amanda was not too sure about the girl, but thought it was probably a case of sisterly protectiveness. 'They're coming, though I thought they'd prefer to spend time together. After all, they are very newly wed.'

Joe was behind her, his arms hugging her to him.

'But not that young. We got together when you were barely twenty-one, remember?'

' 'Course I do.'

Neither mentioned her previous marriage, at seventeen, Joe because he seemed to have forgotten there had ever been another man, Amanda because she never did mention Michael's name between Thursday and Monday.

'I was only twenty-four. A lifetime away. What babies we were.' He brushed his lips gently down her neck. 'Come on, put that tea-towel down and let's go into the sitting-room. I can't talk to you properly when your hands are occupied. We'll both do that, later.' He took the towel from her unresisting grasp and draped it over the oven door.

'Joe . . .' Amanda looked at her husband helplessly, beginning to laugh. 'That's better,' said Joe complacently. 'Do you remember . . .' and he began reminiscing.

In the middle of the night Amanda woke up with a jolt, her heart pounding. Carefully she rolled over on to her back. One of the minor problems of having a husband home only between Thursday and Monday was the sleeping bit. Most of

19

the time she fell asleep immediately after they had made love (to which she looked forward, and was rarely disappointed) and most of the time she slept until the alarm went. There were those occasions, though, when she could only sleep for an hour or so at a time. Then she had to be careful not to wake Joe who hated it if she got up, even if it was merely to make herself a cup of herbal tea.

Indigestion; she supposed that was the cause this time, for they had also eaten steak, and finished a bottle of wine between them. There were other worries: Simon, her job. There was Joe himself. She could text him during the week and he would return her call in the evening, if he wasn't too busy, but she could never phone him directly. Old women did get strange fancies, she understood that, but an intense antipathy towards the telephone?

Amanda turned over cautiously. It was the Rachmaninov, or rather it was that odd dedication, *And to my other family. . . .* She wondered who that other family was, what the woman would think about it, if she knew the music was being played for her. Both women? Now there was a thought. Camomile tea, she decided resolutely. That's what she needed.

'You awake?' Joe murmured. His arm came round her, his hand finding her breast. 'I miss this. I love you.'

No camomile tea, then.

'Mm,' she agreed more than willingly, and slipped into his arms.

Chapter Two

Sara

Joe Williams was a punctual man. Always. Promptly at 7.30 a.m. on this Monday morning, he kissed his wife, Amanda, on the cheek, told her he'd see her on Thursday and let himself out of the house. He drove to the nearest newsagent, after which, as it was a fine day, he made his way to his favourite lock on the Monmouthshire and Brecon Canal where he could park and either read the paper he'd bought or go for a walk on the towpath. When it was very cold or wet, he drove to a nearby truckers' café to sit in its warmth.

At 9.05 (the traffic having been slow because of a breakdown at a set of traffic lights) he took out a treacle tart in a food container concealed under the rug in the boot and pushed his key into the lock of the front door of 29, The Lindens. 'I'm home, Sara,' he called. 'Sorry I'm late. The traffic was diabolical this morning.'

A small bundle of denim and brown curls hurtled out of the kitchen and grabbed his legs, chanting:

'Daddy. Daddy. Daddy. Where've you been?'

He knelt down to hug her, then he picked her up. 'Hello, Nicola. Where's Mummy, pet?' he asked, brushing the hair out of her eyes.

21

'She's on the telephone.' Large blue eyes regarded him solemnly. 'Why're you late, Daddy?'

Joe carried the four-year-old through to the kitchen where her mother, a small woman whose vivacity and charm belied her thirty-six years, was putting down the receiver.

'That was the High Hollows manager,' she said. 'I told him you'd call back later.'

'Sorry I'm late. Bloody slow going this morning.' Joe put down the child and went over to his wife to hug her and kiss her warmly on the lips.

'Poor you. Still, getting up at five a.m. isn't so bad this time of year. And you're only a few minutes late. Did you have a good weekend? And how is Aunt Ethel?' Her eyes were sparkling and there was a becoming flush on her cheekbones, which made him want to kiss her again.

'As well as can be expected,' he said, when he had. 'Aunt Ethel, I mean. She sent you this.' He put the tart, carefully wrapped in foil in the food container to preserve its freshness, on to the table in front of her.

'She really shouldn't, in her state of health. It's far more bother than the fruit-cake she baked last week. But do thank her. I've made some fresh coffee. Like some?'

'Please. Children behaved themselves?'

'Oh yes. Oh, no, Nicola. Take your fingers out of the Marmite. Now look. It's all over your face, and we have to leave in five minutes.'

Nicola, whose thumb had been transferring Marmite from the open jar to her mouth, said stubbornly:

'Don't want to go to nursery school. Want to stay home with my daddy.'

'How about an ice cream after nursery school?' said Joe, benignly.

'Joe, you spoil her.'

'And you read to me?' Nicola held out with all the feminine

wiles of which she was capable.

'And I read to you later,' Joe agreed solemnly.

'Thank you, Joe,' Sara sighed with relief, while their daughter did a hop and a skip. 'I've a load of shopping to do besides going to the launderette. The washing-machine's stopped spinning.'

'I hope you've sent for the engineer,' Joe said. 'But unless it's something easy to fix you'll need a new one with this family to manage.' Then he asked: 'Any messages before you go?'

'It's all right, dear. The man's coming tomorrow. There are three messages. All on your desk, in the study. Come on, now, Nicola. Let me wipe your face and you can kiss Daddy good-bye. I'll take her, throw the stuff in at the launderette and come straight back, if you don't mind coping with her later on?'

'Sure. I'll do the telephoning first, then some dictating. 'Bye chicken. See you soon.' He ruffled Nicola's curls, picked up his coffee-cup and retired to his study. As he closed the door, he heard his daughter ask plaintively, and not for the first time:

'Mummy, why does Daddy always have to go away?' He waited for his wife's patient answer which came as usual:

'Hush, child. Grown-ups often have to do things they would rather not. Now, come along, do, or we'll be dreadfully late.'

Having dropped off her daughter, Sara Williams sat in the empty car listening to the closing moments of Rachmaninov's second piano concerto on Classic FM – which she'd also heard only the previous afternoon. What was it the DJ had said at the end? Something about a dedication, *And for my other family*. . . . It had intrigued her then and now it set her thinking about the question Nicola asked every Monday morning to which she had replied as usual: *Grown-ups often have to do things they'd rather not.*

They had met eighteen years ago, she and Joe. Joe made and sold agricultural machinery. They had fallen in love conventionally, over walks in the park and evenings in the local wine-bar. She found him wildly exciting with his dark, good looks and his passionate kisses, which still managed to convey that she was something special. Joe was her first serious boyfriend. She had been kissed before — but found the young men clumsy, their wet lips repulsive in a way that surprised her. Joe was different. She had caught her breath when she saw him, lost herself in his dark eyes. Frequently he told her he found her adorable, trustingly naïve, but quite adorable.

It was not until her eighteenth birthday that Sara realized there was anything at all about Joe that was different from other men. Her parents had planned a party on the Saturday. It was to be just a small party but she had bought a new, daringly cut, black dress and booked a hair appointment to have the ends of her long, dark hair trimmed. Naturally Joe was invited. He declined. It was not that he did not want to come, he insisted, his hand caressingly on the side of her face, his thumb gently rubbing her ear-lobe. Any weekday, he said, but he always spent Thursdays to Mondays with his Aunt Ethel, who did not enjoy the best of health. She knew, of course, that he had two businesses? The second was nominally Aunt Ethel's. He always had to put in a full day on Friday at the family works and he did the paper work on Saturdays.

How could he do this to her? Sara could not understand it. Why wouldn't he make an exception? Surely his aunt would understand this was for something special? She was shocked, hurt, confused, and told him so. She'd thought she was special to him. Joe was adamant. 'You are special, but I can't come to the party.' She burst into tears and vowed she'd never see him again.

A few weeks later, with the quarrel made up, Joe asked casually:

'Come away with me this weekend?'

'What do you mean?' She knew, of course, but people, girls like her, didn't do that sort of thing. Then. 'You're not suggesting . . .'

'That we spend time with each other. We don't get much of that, do we, alone? We could go to the Lake District.'

'We see each other several times a week.'

'That's not what I meant, Sara.'

'I – I thought you were coming to love me, not that you just wanted to take me to bed. I thought there was some future in our relationship.'

'I want to take you to bed, all right,' he said, catching her to him and kissing her so that for several minutes she forgot what they had been discussing. 'I think I am falling in love with you, but I shall never ask you to marry me, because I don't believe in it.'

'In marriage?' she asked, aghast. 'Everyone believes in marriage.'

'I've seen too many come adrift. When I know I love someone I'll make a commitment – for as long as that love lasts. Just don't ask for more.'

Sara didn't go away with him, but over the next couple of months they talked and argued, kissed and caressed until she was dizzy with desire and half-mad from frustration, and she cried and still there seemed no way out.

It was Sara who eventually suggested that they should just live together, that in effect she should become his common-law wife. The audacity of it quite confounded her when she looked back now at that time. She must have been mad: that is, not insane but quite crazy to suggest such a thing, and mean it.

'I think we should compromise,' she said. 'Live together. The commitment would be there. The only thing lacking would be the piece of paper.' She saw a tremor run through Joe as she spoke and thought only that he was amazed by her daring.

At first he did seem utterly shocked.

'Live with me? I don't see how. I couldn't ask it of you.' But he had. It had not taken her so very long to convince him.

A few weeks later Joe told Sara, 'I've worked out that I've enough for the down payment on a house for us. That is, if you're quite sure you understand about my commitments to Aunt Ethel.'

'Oh, Joe!' Sara fell into his arms, covered his face with kisses and allowed him a small intimacy that she had so far steadfastly withheld, whispering only that she did hope he would keep her a virgin until their wedding night.

'As long as you promise never to blame me for the lack of a wedding ceremony,' Joe replied shakily.

They staged an elopement. They told her parents they were going on holiday together. A couple of weeks in Benidorm, they said. Mr and Mrs Moody sniffed and both secretly hoped the two would take care, a great deal of care. It was not to Benidorm they flew, but Antigua, where Joe knew they could stage the elopement that never was. A little money hired the wedding finery, paid the photographer. From there they duly telephoned her parents with the news that they had been married – to avoid the sort of family fuss they both would have hated, they declared. Mrs Moody wept over the phone and Mr Moody was irate. Both so-called newly weds dreaded the coming encounter once they were home.

It was not as bad as they feared. 'I hope you'll both be very happy,' Mrs Moody sniffed.

'There was a time, young man, when it was customary to ask permission of the father,' Mr Moody said ponderously.

'Oh, Dad,' said Sara.

'Well, there it is.'

As everything else seemed above board – the photos of the happy couple were duly admired in their album – Sara's parents continued to express their dismay and disappointment in no uncertain terms for a week or two, but never did ask to see her marriage lines. Two months later the parents set about forgiving the errant pair with a handsome cheque and Mrs Moody's mother's canteen of Edwardian silver cutlery.

So there never had been a wedding. Why had she gone ahead with it? Why had she accepted what many would have called second best. Because it never had been second best, not for Sara. She loved Joe, loved him for his looks, for the way he made her feel, for the way he never stopped caring for her welfare.

Yet she did recognize that it was a strange relationship, outwardly like so many others, but with areas that Sara was forbidden to enter. Monday to Thursday Joe lived with her, worked in his study, went to the works, had business meetings. Was there. But at midday on Thursday he left. Christmas, the children's holidays, no matter what, he went. There was one week in the year when they all went away together (and one week in the year when he did not come home at all because of a conference he attended in London). And that was her marriage.

'I can't think why you don't sell the old lady's house, buy something bigger and have her to live with you,' Mrs Moody once snorted. 'Then Joe could work nine to five like any normal man and not leave you to cope on your own. It isn't right.'

Except for the fact that Sara was very glad not to be faced with an unknown, frail old lady, she was inclined to agree with her mother. There were times, too, when she had been almost convinced in her own mind that Joe went off to another woman. Yet his behaviour to herself, especially his sexual need of her, was such that she did not see how there could be another woman, except Aunt Ethel. There had

certainly been none of the classic evidence of such an involve-
ment – lipstick on the collar, perfume on his clothes, a strange
handkerchief in his pocket. If Aunt Ethel was a myth, the
myth was solidly constructed indeed. *And for my other
family.* . . . She supposed there must be no end of households
to which that applied.

'Found the messages all right, love?' Sara asked when she
arrived home. She leaned over the desk beside her husband.

'Sure. I've finished the letters, too. Just got to drop the tape
into the office this afternoon. Do the usual rounds tomorrow.
Nicola go off all right, little monkey?' He scribbled a note, put
down his pen and flexed his fingers, a smile on his lips and in
his voice.

'Yes. She always does. You know that.' There was a tight-
ness in Sara's throat and she swallowed. It was absurd, she
was thinking. *Almost as if it was the first time and I was
nervous.* As her fingers tightened in the thick hair at the nape
of his neck he murmured into her heated flesh:

'I've missed you, my dearest love.'

Then he rose, swept her into his arms (since she was still
light and he was in good shape) and carried her into the
sitting-room. As he placed her on the sofa and took off his
already loosened tie he said, 'It's such a long time from
Thursday to Monday,' his tone so urgent, his gaze so magnetic
that all thoughts of shopping and laundry were forgotten. Joe
was home.

'It's choir practice tonight, Mum,' Harriet bounced into the
kitchen as Sara was stirring beaten eggs and milk into a
bread-and-butter pudding. 'You won't forget my tea, will you?'
Harriet had recently joined the local church, rather to her
parents' surprise, for the family usually only went at
Christmas, but Harriet's current best friend went to church
regularly, and she had an elder brother who was fancied by

the more impressionable girls in Harriet's class.

'I'll meet you outside the church at nine o'clock,' said her father.

'Oh, Dad,' wailed Harriet. 'We want to go for a coffee.'

'Homework?' asked Sara.

'Done that, Mum. At school.'

'Any school that permits homework to be done there isn't doing its job properly,' pontificated Joe.

'Dad, you are old-fashioned,' Harriet began. 'I had a study period,' she ended, her voice sulky.

'Half-past nine, then, and not a moment later,' he declared firmly.

'Oh, thanks, Dad. You're a doll.' She scurried from the room.

'Mm. Might have to watch that one for a bit.'

Sara was watching him with what he would have called her wifely look, if he had noticed it. She forbore to mention that she had been thinking about Harriet for some months with considerable maternal anxiety.

'I shouldn't worry about it, love,' she said, calmly enough. 'Harriet may be your typically infuriating teenager. She's a sensible girl underneath it all.'

Nicola had been trying to attract Joe's attention for five minutes.

'Dolly's lost her eyes again. You can put it right, can't you, Daddy?' A tear rolled down her woebegone face. Joe could always be relied on when it came to minute anatomical repairs. He bent down obediently to comfort the child and with a tweak the doll was mended and restored to Nicola's arms.

At supper time Harriet strolled downstairs.

'Mum. Whatever've you done with my new top?' she complained, as she sat down at the kitchen table. 'It's baggy.'

Joe was leaning against the wall, a glass of wine in his hand, watching his wife slice bread. Now he straightened.

'That's not baggy,' he said, as he took in her lilac camisole top with shoe-string straps, 'it's shrunk.'

'Dad. It's supposed to be fitted.'

'It shows your belly-button. And what on earth have you got there?'

Harriet rolled her eyes. 'Belly-button. Dad, that's Jurassic.'

'You've pierced your navel.'

'Oh, Harriet, no,' her mother said. 'It's terribly unhygienic. Besides, I thought you'd agreed that you wouldn't provided we allowed you to have your ears pierced for your next birthday.'

'It's only a stick-on jewel,' Harriet said sullenly. 'Honestly, anyone would think I've committed a crime.'

'It's still indecent,' roared her father. 'Go and cover yourself up. I can't understand why you don't wear a nice skirt and blouse.'

Sara took pity on her overtaxed husband.

'Yes. Well, if it really is only a stick-on, I suppose it doesn't matter. But not for everyday, and certainly not for school. Now, do eat your tea or you'll be late.'

Joe had been thrilled when his daughter, Harriet, now just sixteen, was born. She was a brunette like her mother and he spoiled her outrageously. Sara always wanted a large family but to their disappointment she had not become pregnant again until, totally unexpectedly when Harriet was eleven, she conceived. David was the result. After David's birth Joe had assumed responsibility for contraception. Both he and Sara thought that another few years would pass before she conceived again, if she ever did, so neither was too bothered about the occasional lapse. They were astounded when she conceived little more than a year after Davids' first birthday, but when Nicola arrived he adored her, too.

They had been forced to move, though, and home was now a Georgian terraced house, convenient for the factory which was on the outskirts of Cwmbran, a sprawling industrial town in east Gwent. They were near enough to the real country, Black Mountains and Brecon Beacons, for walks and picnics and occasionally even the Gower coast in high summer. Sara was amazed when Joe insisted this house should be in her name alone.

'Purely a matter of insurance,' he told her. 'You never know, these days.'

'It doesn't seem quite right, but if you insist.'

'All a matter of high finance, the accountant told me. So let's take his word for it, shall we, mm?'

It was typical of Joe, a little overbearing, but so kind with it, and of course he was a few years older than she was, and there were the children to consider, should anything ever happen to him. But it was no wonder she loved him dearly.

By the following afternoon, Sara's mood had altered completely. Nicola and Davey were almost unmanageable. Whatever one picked up, the other wanted. Whatever one said, the other contradicted, louder. In the end she lost her temper with them both.

'Upstairs,' she yelled. 'You'll get no tea if I hear one more sound out of either of you!' They fled.

Harriet sauntered into the kitchen.

'Mum. Have you seen my pink top?'

'No. I have not,' snapped Sara. 'If you were a sight tidier you'd be able to find your own things instead of worrying me for them.'

'Sorry I spoke,' Harriet answered insolently, and turned on her heel. Sara could have slapped her.

'Come back here,' she shouted. Harriet obeyed, looking a little abashed. Sara made herself relax. 'Sorry,' she apologized in her turn. 'I didn't mean to scream at you. Look, I think your pink sweater is on Nicola's table. Go and quieten those two,

31

will you? I can't stand much more. Your dad'll be home soon and just see this mess.'

For a moment it seemed that there was to be a confrontation. Then Harriet thought better of it. She turned back to her mother, sighing.

'If I look after the brats can I stay out for an extra hour?'

'Half an hour,' said Sara, automatically entering into bargaining mode.

'Oh, all right, then. And if you see my pink . . . look, there isn't much of a mess, really. I'll take the ironing up with me, shall I?'

'Thanks, dear,' said Sara, knowing that Harriet understood that it was not just for the ironing.

The fact was that Sara was preoccupied. She had tidied the bathroom cabinet while Joe was working only to discover that her packet of the pill was two bubbles out. Guilt nagged her. It was so unlike her to be careless now that she knew just how fertile she was. She had stayed up to watch late-night TV twice, but that was no excuse. So why had she forgotten? Moreover, it would be just her luck if Joe had already made her pregnant.

Joe, entering the kitchen noiselessly, dropped a kiss on the back of his wife's neck, startling her. The result was electric. Sara squealed, dropped the cup she was washing up and broke it.

'Now look what you've made me do,' she cried, her cheeks flushed with exasperation.

'Hey. Hey! What is this? Fine reception a man gets for a small kiss, I must say.'

Sara burst into tears. Joe put his arms round her immediately and she buried her face in his shoulder. Not for the world could, or would, she tell him the half of what was really bothering her.

'Come on, now,' he cajoled her. 'It was only a small cup . . .

like the small kiss . . . joke?' he said plaintively. Sara smiled wanly but he could feel it through his cashmere sweater, the sudden movement as her lips curled upwards.

'What Mum needs is a holiday,' Harriet observed shrewdly, coming on the scene. 'She's all on edge.'

'Oh now, I don't know about that,' Joe answered uneasily.

'That's what Mary said this morning when I took Nicola to school.' Mary was a neighbour. Sara lifted her tear-blotched face to Joe. She had never been able to cry without her face looking a mess. She remembered that belatedly and buried herself in his sweater again. Besides, the softness of the wool was comforting.

'If it's nerves perhaps you should go to the doctor,' Joe suggested. 'I expect he could give you something to calm you down.'

The inference that what she needed was a pill was enough to send Sara headlong into floods of tears once more.

'I don't want a pill,' she sniffled, 'I want . . . I want . . .' She stopped. Almost her heart stopped. What she had almost said was, *I want a baby.* She hiccupped. 'A holiday,' she ended feebly.

'Well.' Joe drew out the word, looking from wife to daughter. 'A holiday, eh? Well, why not? I suppose it is the time of the year for sorting out the family holiday. I'd better do something about it.'

A week or so later Joe announced that they were spending their summer holiday on a narrow-boat in the Midlands. To say that Sara was dumbfounded would have been an understatement.

'You're mad,' she said, all the alternatives flashing through her mind in quick succession. 'Have you ever been on a narrow-boat before? No,' she answered herself. 'And where did you say we'd go? The Midlands. The weather's bound to be awful.'

It was not what she wanted at all. Given her choice, Sara would have liked to go back to Menorca. But they went abroad every other year, so she knew it would have to be somewhere in the UK. All right, so she would have preferred a self-catering cottage by the sea, with central heating and a washing-machine. Somewhere safe for the children to play in rock pools. Somewhere with a little night-life so that she and Joe could eat out once or twice. Somewhere with a bit of dancing. But a narrow-boat?

'It'll be different. Look.' He produced a brochure, opening it at a page showing an idyllic family scene, playful children, refulgent sun and dappled shade. 'Don't you think the boat looks charming, painted flowers along its sides – look at the checked curtains. Besides, it's got all the mod cons. Central heating, too.'

As if flowers or curtains made that much of a difference in the wet, for it was absolutely bound to rain. Reluctantly Sara picked up the brochure and flicked through it.

'It looks really hard work, going through a lock. How many do you think there are?'

Joe shrugged, 'Oh, Davey and I'll manage those, won't we, son?'

'No sweat,' said David.

'David,' chorused his parents.

'Besides, I thought we'd ask your father to join us. You know how much Henry enjoys a week away from his sister occasionally.'

Sara was mollified. Widowed, her father now lived in Yorkshire with his spinster sister. The two got on together really well, considering, but she knew how much her father loved visiting his only grandchildren.

Joe's enthusiasm was infectious. As he continued to paint Sara a picture of warm days, flower-scented meadows, of merry boatloads of canalers gliding down tranquil stretches of water before tying up at quaint canalside pubs, lock gates opening at a touch and everyone helping with the washing-up, she allowed herself to be convined.

'I've requested life-jackets for the children,' said Joe. 'No sense in asking for trouble. But Henry'll be there to keep an eye on them. You'll see. It'll be marvelous. We'll have the greatest fun!'

Two weeks before the holiday, Sara bought a pregnancy test kit. She kept it for several days before she actually used it, knowing that the whole excercise was a waste of time, but dreading what it would reveal. It was positive, as she had known it would be. It seemed almost pointless to bother the doctor, but he was very nice about it and immediately set about organizing the usual proceedures.

Now all that remained was to tell Joe he was to become a father for the fourth time.

Chapter Three

Joe on Joe

I never set out to have two families. You have to believe that. I never thought of myself as a philanderer, still less an adulterer.

I am an only child. My father, an engineer, was killed in an industrial accident when I was five. I adored my mother who died tragically young from cancer, when she was only forty-five, so you could say that I have had to be tough and single-minded all my life. I suppose you could say that this story begins a year or so after my mother's death when I met Amanda. At the time I was twenty-four. I was a reasonably tall, reasonably well-built man in good health and of sound mind (probably a middling sort of man when it comes down to it, though I also thought of myself as a snazzy dresser), with brown eyes and plenty of hair (which I've kept). Despite the way in which my father died, I took a degree in engineering and with little difficulty I gained excellent experience in industry with a good firm. I liked my life and I intended to stay carefree for a good few years.

I met Amanda one evening at a club in Croydon. She was absolutely gorgeous, vivacious, dressed to kill, half a head shorter than me, with straight, dark hair and brown eyes. She has always hated her nose, but I thought then, and still do, that it gives character to her face. I wanted her from the first moment I saw her and it appeared she felt the same way about me. What started out as a chance encounter became a full-on relationship immediately. I think it surprised both of us that it happened quite so quickly. But it was much, much more than a matter of congratulating myself on my pulling powers. That whole evening had something magical about it, as if it had been meant from the start. Fanciful? Maybe.

After that first night, every moment I could, I saw her. Also, after that first time I was careful, so when Amanda told me she was pregnant I think my first reaction was indignation. Typical male, do I hear you sneer? You are probably right. But in the same moment I knew that there could not have been anyone else. There was absolutely no question of blame, the baby had to be mine. What was more, pride, smugness, conceit, call it what you will, filled me. We had made a baby. Wow.

Then, like a revelation, I knew that we had to do the thing properly and set up house together. So it happened more rapidly than I had planned. I had found someone I loved and if the family I had always wanted came along sooner than was ideal, in my orphaned state that was no bad thing.

Do the thing properly, I hear you ask? Set up house together? No mention, then, of any marriage?

No. I explained all this very carefully to Amanda. There's something about marriage that scares the shit out of me. Always has. Ah, because of your father, I imagine the amateur psychologists among you argue, death being abandonment to a five-year-old. That has nothing to do with it. I like to think I've never broken a promise. The marriage ceremony demands promises that are wholly unrealistic, if you ask me. I promised Amanda that I'd live with her and bring up our children for as long as we continued to love each other. As far as I was concerned, I hoped that would be for ever.

You never know what's round the corner.

37

I was a bit surprised about Amanda's divorce. There you are, she'd married him too young. She said he was violent. She was well shot of him, if you ask me. But isn't that just what I've been saying? They made a promise they couldn't keep. I suppose that at least made me appreciate her parents' point of view, for they were a bit sniffy at first, but that was entirely normal for the times. One marriage ending in disaster was bad enough, a second with a man they had only just met was a dire prospect.

It so happened that my mother's estate had just finished probate. There had been a good insurance and compensation package when my father died which had been invested well in its time. I had found a run-down factory, in Cwmbran in SE Wales, which seemed to me to have prospects. I knew what I was doing. I knew I could make a go of it, making spare parts for agricultural machinery. It just meant that I had to relocate from London to Cwmbran.

Of course it took some cajoling to convince Amanda. This wasn't a thing most people did in those days, setting up home together. If I'm honest, there was an element of emotional blackmail, now I come to think about it, but after the initial shock had worn off she seemed happy enough, and when her parents (who I know were appalled) learnt that we were moving some 150 miles away they seemed relieved, if anything.

Those first months, the move, the upheaval of taking over the plant, was hard work, but it was exhilarating. I've always thrived on challenges. When Simon was born I thought I'd been given the world. He was amazing, perfectly healthy, with everything in the right place, lots of dark hair but with my looks (Amanda said). I was so proud, I strutted.

The feeling lasted for about the first two months of his life as I bent over his crib, making plans for the rest of his life. You know the sort of thing?

Then the terror swamped me.

It didn't even come gradually. One minute I was really pleased and happy, the next I was filled with dread. I might drop him. His little body seemed not to grow more sturdy, rather it felt as precious as porcelain, and equally vulnerable. Suddenly I was scared to touch him, filled with fear that some act of mine would take him from us. I was petrified that we would never be able to raise him to adulthood, that we could never afford the things that he would need.

Why didn't I tell Amanda? I was frightened of what she would say. You see, she was incredible. She'd been so brave during the birth, she seemed, no, she *was* so capable afterwards. She made me feel utterly inferior.

Then the letter from Aunt Ethel arrived. It was providential. I really only intended visiting for one night, make soothing noises and return home immediately. Aunt Ethel was my only living relation, a second cousin.

Aunt Ethel had been very good to my mother when she was a child and even when my mother died I kept in touch – the cards at Christmas and her birthday, an occasional telephone call, an infrequent visit. Aunt Ethel had been a widow for many years. Her husband, who I always thought was a bit feckless, had left her a light-engineering firm, manufacturing parts for agricultural machines, which, like my own, was in need of updating. The factory was in Bromsgrove. Aunt Ethel was in failing health and had decided to make me her heir. She had a perfectly competent manager and all the plant needed was an injection of cash to bring it back to real profit. She wanted me to see if there was any way in which I could invest in it to make the inheritance worthwhile.

It certainly wasn't a decision to be made overnight.

I honestly thought I had to refuse. But there was this thing about family life that had got to me. The messiness of babies, the stinking nappies, the regurgitated milk, took me by surprise. I felt side-lined, too, by my own wife. It seemed as though she didn't need me any more, unless it was to walk a wailing baby in the night, just when I was craving sleep. I know. Every father feels that way, just as every mother is overwhelmed by the time and energy the newborn require.

The answer to my problems was there, staring me in the face. I could save my sanity. I could do what I knew I should do for Aunt Ethel – a small investment not being too impossible at that time. As a by-product, so to speak, I could provide even more generously for my family, if I worked hard and made a success of both works.

There was no intention of abandoning Amanda and Simon. You have to believe that. I loved Amanda, have never ceased loving her. And Simon worked his own long-distance magic. I missed him – them – more than I imagined it was possible. I knew I needed them as much as they needed me.

I returned home and told Amanda what I proposed and I embarked on the first of my lies. Lies work best when they are grounded in truth. I told Amanda that Aunt Ethel wanted me to manage the plant, to rescue it before it was too late and there was nothing to leave. I made it sound as though the whole idea was hers.

'You want us to move. Again? To Bromsgrove?'

'I want, need, to keep both factories open. (That was true enough.) I want to spend one part of the week with Aunt Ethel, the rest with you and Simon.' And held my breath.

Amanda took two days to think it through. In the end she agreed. I think I was so grateful that my plan was working that it never occurred to me to wonder why she would even contemplate the suggestion. It also never occurred to me that I might have diminished her in any way. Indeed, very soon after, with her figure fully regained, her composure undimmed, she was breathtaking. I left her on Mondays with real regret.

But leave I did. Monday to Thursday I spent with Aunt Ethel, coming and going as I wanted. Thursday afternoons I arrived in Chestnut Drive, spending Friday at my own Cwmbran plant. It worked. We never quarrelled, our relationship became even stronger. I loved Amanda very much and told her so, frequently.

On the practical side, I made sure Amanda had help in the house. I bought her a small car and gave her a generous allowance. Later, when he was three, Simon was enrolled in the best local nursery school.

Then Aunt Ethel confounded me by dying. I was in a quandary. What was I to do? Tell Amanda, sell the house, abandon my freedom? And what about the second factory? I really didn't want to get rid of that because it was beginning to make a healthy profit. I thought, what was the point of changing anything? I installed a housekeeper and continued as before. The point was though, that while I slept in Aunt Ethel's house, inevitably I had a lot of time on my own.

I forgot to mention that I believe Aunt Ethel tended to feel sorry for Amanda. With hindsight I think she must have felt that I should have brought Amanda and Simon to Bromsgrove, even if it was not to her immaculate house. Whenever she could, she used to bake something for her which I would take home. When she became frailer, she persuaded me to call at the WI stall on a Thursday morning. There was this woman who baked the most amazing treacle tarts you've ever tasted. She said she used wholemeal breadcrumbs from bread she'd baked herself. Whatever, it was moist and tangy and altogether delicious. We had it for Sunday lunch and Simon and I almost fought for the last slice. When Aunt Ethel died I just put in a standing order for the treacle tart, alternating it with a fruit cake. Amanda was always very grateful.

As I said, with no responsibilities I had plenty of spare time. It was on one of those evenings that, by accident, I met this woman in the park. I met Sara.

And everything changed.

Chapter Four

Amanda

Amanda had promised to mend a pair of jeans for Simon so Saturday afternoon saw Joe on his own at the cricket ground, watching him take three wickets and scoring a creditable ten runs before being out lbw.

'Good match. He's becoming quite a player, isn't he? Better than I was at his age,' he said to Amanda as they were walking round to spend the evening with friends.

Amanda heard the note of fatherly pride mixed with some middle-aged envy.

'I daresay he's had more chances, with the cricket club and all that.'

'No. It's natural talent.' There was a pause. 'I've not seen that Lindy before. Si's got it made there, all right.'

Amanda frowned. 'What do you mean?'

'You know.' He sketched a female figure in the air with his hands. 'The way she hung on his arm said it all.'

'It's all very well admiring your son's prowess on the cricket field. You might be a bit more careful when it comes to what he does behind the cricket pavilion after dark. Not to mention who he does it with.'

He caught hold of her arm. 'What do you mean, careful?'

'You know very well what I mean. And he knows what I mean when I tell him to be careful,' she replied obliquely. 'I only hope you taught him properly.'

'Amanda' Joe sounded thoroughly shocked. 'You . . . he . . . talking together about – about . . . I don't think that's quite nice.'

Surprise at this quite unexpected reaction rocked her back on her high heels.

'So it's all right for him to be having it off with her, but not to talk about it at home. That's typical of a man. Though I never thought to hear it from you. I'd rather he was open about his girls. That way he's less likely to get one of them pregnant.' *Like you got me.* The thought rang so clearly in her head that Amanda was convinced she'd said it aloud.

'Ssh.' The expression on Joe's face was so horrified as he glanced round hurriedly in case they had been overheard that Amanda swallowed the unexpected resentment and allowed herself a wry smile. She was sure that Joe had forgotten that unplanned pregnancy had ever happened to them. 'I refuse to discuss this further.' He took her arm firmly once more.

'You're an old fraud,' she said fondly, because it had happened so long ago it seemed to be in a different life. She allowed herself to be propelled forward. Then she said: 'I bet you'd feel differently if a daughter of yours was involved.' She stepped off the pavement.

Amanda was thinking that it was not only the problem of Simon's sexuality that worried her. His future was not fully settled, and though it had been discussed when he entered the sixth form she had the distinct feeling that they were in for a rocky ride. She supposed they might return to the matter later on, though somehow the timing was never quite right.

On Sunday, according to custom, Amanda got up at about nine o'clock, made a pot of tea and a pile of buttered toast and took it upstairs on a tray along with the *News Of The World* and the *Sunday Express*. Then she settled herself back against the pillows, the tray between them.

She waited until the tea and toast had gone, the tray was safely on the floor and the sports pages reached. Then she asked abruptly:

'Joe, what do you think is going to happen to Simon after he leaves school?'

'I don't know. Ask him. Ask the school. Did you read this? It says—'

'Please listen. I'm worried about him.'

Joe put down the paper. 'What does the school say?'

'Not much. They say he should get the right grades. You remember he has an offer from a couple of universities? Only, there's the cricket and his music. Has he worked hard enough? And what if he doesn't get the right results? I've tried, really I have, but it all seems very last minute.'

'You worry too much.'

Joe wasn't paying any attention. It was always her responsibility. She sighed and shrugged her shoulders and the strap of the cotton candy-striped vest she wore in bed slipped. Firmly she removed the hand that followed the strap.

'Simon seems quite happy,' she admitted. 'He says he's expecting top grades. It all seems a bit optimistic to me.' There were times when she would have welcomed more obvious support from Simon's father. This was becoming one of them.

Joe had expected the brush-off and did not seem too put out.

'If he says he'll get top grades I don't mind betting that's just what'll happen. What's he intending to do during the summer?'

'He's going to work on a building-site as soon as term's over. He's going to make enough money to buy an old van. Then he's going to do it up for the group—'

'Hold on. Perhaps I do need to talk to him. But later on,'

said Joe, anxious to conclude the conversation, speedily divesting himself of boxer shorts. 'After Sunday lunch. Not now. You weren't thinking of going anywhere, were you?' His hand caressed her bare thigh.

Once again Amanda sighed.

'No, love,' she answered fondly, because when all was said and done this was where she wanted to be. 'Not this morning.'

'I love you.' Her husband lifted his head, his eyes gazing deeply into hers. 'Always remember that. I love you very much.'

'So what's all this about Simon?' It was lunchtime and Joe, who had met John in the pub, was strolling home with him. Joe made no secret of the fact he loved Sundays. 'I was looking forward to reading the papers in peace this afternoon. Suppose I'll have to talk to him instead.'

'I'm sure Amanda worries too much about Simon. Next to his cricket, those drums are his pride and joy. Just don't push him. He'll work things out in his own way, you'll see. There's an awful lot of you in Simon, it seems to me.'

'So I should hope.' Joe chuckled. 'You know, I do worry about them all, now that you're married and living further away. I wouldn't want him to do anything stupid.'

'I wouldn't worry,' said John comfortably. 'There's too much of Amanda in him for that.'

Amanda waved to them through the window and the aromatic smell of roast pork wafted over them.

'I don't suppose there's any real need to say anything to them now,' Joe declared. 'Time enough when it actually happens.'

John hoped he was right. Whatever went wrong in Simon's life was definitely his father's fault, not his mother's. Joe was not one of John's favourite people. For John was one of the few who knew the whole truth about Michael.

45

Amanda had left school at sixteen to go to her local technical college for her A levels with high hopes of doing brilliantly at art and design, finding herself a fantastic job and earning a fabulous salary. Within a few weeks she had met Michael, a newly qualified accountant, at a local wine bar. He was with a group of older, racier, students but before the end of the evening they had quietly slipped away together and from then on they were inseparable. Then Michael was offered a job in the Midlands. As it seemed inconceivable that they should part, he asked her to marry him.

Her parents were horrified: she was too young, she would be leaving college without qualifications. From the beginning they had never really thought he was right for her. They begged and pleaded but eventually the marriage was arranged. Would they have been the last to say, *we told you so* when it proved a disaster from the wedding night? Fearing their reaction, Amanda never told them the half of it. Michael, too nervous – and too drunk – to recognize a similar state in his virgin wife, first hit her then forcibly penetrated her when she suggested timidly that she preferred to go to sleep rather than have the sex he was wanting.

The next day, bruised and bewildered, Amanda took refuge in a sulky silence which continued when Michael retaliated by alternately ignoring her and demanding what he called his rights. By the end of the honeymoon they were scarcely speaking.

At home, they soon ceased to worry about what the neighbours might think; he shouted and she slammed doors until, goaded by an indiscreet remark, Michael hit her again. She cowered, and he began to despise her for not standing up to him. In the weeks that followed, the more she cringed, the more sadistic enjoyment he got from unleashed violence.

Within months he was beating her regularly.

Amanda stood it for a year before leaving him. Michael, hurt and angry, found her going back to a women's refuge from a shopping-trip. He dragged her home and broke a couple of her ribs. She waited until they healed, then she left him again. This time she was more cautious over her expeditions from the refuge she had found in Birmingham. This time Michael did not bother to look for her. Sickened and scared by his own behaviour, he sought counselling and eventually agreed they were best apart.

Like many women in similar circumstances, Amanda had kept this from her parents, made easier because for the past three winters they had eked out their pensions in a small apartment in Malta. John, a few years older than Amanda, knew about Michael almost from the start, for he had visited his sister unexpectedly while he was on leave and found her covered with bruises. Fiercely protective of her marriage, she vowed him to secrecy.

Once she had left Michael for good, Amanda moved south, to Croydon and a bed-sit, to be nearer her parents. At that stage there was no talk even of a judicial separation. She was just glad to be away from him. Her parents did not like it, but she had the feeling that they were relieved to be spared the embarrassment of having her at home. Now, without the formal qualifications for the sort of job she would have preferred, she went to work in a supermarket. Shortly after she started work, Amanda met Joe.

She confessed to John, one Christmas night, what had really happened, both with Michael and with Joe. John had come home from Africa where he was working. They were sitting on the hearthrug in front of the glowing embers of a coal fire. Simon was in bed. Joe was away. Tipsy on ginger wine, Amanda told him that Joe would decline to celebrate Christmas with them again until the festival fell once more at the weekend.

'What on earth is he doing, then?'

'Oh, you know. Spending it with Aunt Ethel, when he isn't working.'

It was on the tip of John's tongue to suggest that they should buy a bigger house which would accommodate Aunt Ethel, too. Then he realized that maybe Amanda wouldn't care to have to look after Aunt Ethel.

'He—he doesn't . . .' John began, then stopped.

'No. He hasn't another woman,' Amanda replied quite calmly, for even she had to admit that it was a logical suggestion, coming from another man. 'Don't you think I would be the first to find out if he had? I'm not stupid, you know, and a woman can always tell if she isn't the only one in a man's life,' she went on a little fiercely, as if she was trying to convince herself as well as her brother.

'Yes, I understand that,' interrupted John, who wasn't really sure that he did, or that she was right in her assumption. But he had nothing to go on himself and was sure he was in deep enough already in her emotional life. He thought it would be a lot better if he heard no more details.

'Let me tell you about my life,' Amanda urged, her hand gripping his knee firmly. 'What it's like with Joe. What it's like to have him home . . . and what it's like when he's not here.'

And she had, down to the details which it was probably lucky she had forgotten, by the morning, that she had ever divulged. John was convinced, despite himself.

'I don't understand him, though,' he said doggedly, when she had finished.

'Does anyone?' Amanda agreed, with the only touch of bitterness he ever heard from her. 'While Aunt Ethel lives and Joe has his work, we are a weekend family. Like it or not. And most of the time I do. I don't understand Joe, I just love him. Most of the time . . .' she repeated owlishly. 'I thought I loved Michael, but I was so young. We both were. Far too young.

48

Love is wasted on the young, they say.'

'I thought that was youth.'

'Anyway, our relationship hadn't a hope from the beginning. But Joe is different. He loves me. I know that. And I love him.'

At tea-time Joe saw the brochure, left carelessly on the sofa in Chestnut Way, the small, detached house in a 1970s cul-de-sac in Cwmbran, the town in east Gwent. The brochure advertised canal holidays in narrow boats.

'Where did you get this?' he demanded.

'Mum found it underneath your bedside table,' said Simon. 'We thought you must have sent for it for our summer holiday. It would be good fun if we all did something like this again.'

'All of us? You insisted on giving up family holidays three years ago.'

'Yes, but that was because I went camping with John instead and John has Fay now.'

'Well, obviously another holiday together would be good,' Joe agreed, sounding cautious. 'But have you thought of the weather?' he demanded repressively. 'Actually a friend of mine gave this to me, thought I might be interested. I read it, but I can't say I think much of the idea. It seems to me the Med would be a far better prospect for us.'

'Oh, not just lying on the beach, Dad. Boring. . . .'

'We'll see. I'll think about it again. You'd like to go abroad, wouldn't you, dear?' he asked Amanda, who had just come into the room.

'Oh, Joe, yes please.' She became aware of an atmosphere. 'Have I missed something?'

'Not really, Mum,' Simon replied. 'We were just talking about holidays, generally, you know.'

'Ah.' Holidays were always a tricky subject with Joe. He liked to alternate between a holiday in the UK and somewhere abroad. The previous year he had taken her to Skye.

She'd loved that. But she had missed Simon. Of course the Mediterranean would be lovely, though she could see that her son was of an age to prefer something more energetic than just lying on a beach, eyeing the girls. He needed something more active. Like the narrow-boat on a canal they'd mentioned after she'd found the brochure by Joe's side of the bed. Might Joe compromise? Take a narrow-boat on a French canal? She'd have to work on it.

'I'll think of something,' said Joe. 'Just leave it with me.'

Amanda stared reflectively after her husband as he left the room. She grinned at the disconsolate Simon.

'You know your father. Never mind. We'll see what we can sort out, shall we? After all, the summer's a good few weeks, from start to finish.' She had missed seeing the pleasure on her son's face these past few years, missed hearing his enthusiasm as they holidayed together. Though she was realist enough to know that the generations couldn't always relax companionably together. She had a bit of her own money saved up, and if she liked to spend it on a holiday with her son there was not much Joe could complain about. If she even told him. After all, there was no point in upsetting him needlessly. They could still also go where he wanted to take them. 'We'll talk about it later, shall we, my love?'

After Joe had left for work on Monday morning, Amanda hunted for the narrow-boat brochure and found it under the pile of discarded Sunday papers. She began to read it. That evening over tea she broached the matter.

'It'd have to be when Joe is in London at the annual conference,' she said. 'There's no point in upsetting your father unnecessarily.'

Simon nodded sagely. There were things they kept from Joe. They did not set out to deceive him, but there were events and occurrences they did not mention. It might be a school function which they knew he would be disappointed to miss, outings during the school holidays. After all, he was away for most of the week. It was not unreasonable to make plans that excluded his father. Conspiratorially, they agreed that this was an occasion when they would do what they wanted to do, and to preserve the peace, Joe need never know.

'The London conference is the usual time, the third week in July,' Amanda said. It was the first time she had ever considered actually going away without Joe. It was rather exciting, something of an adventure.

'You can have my youth-hostelling money, Mum.'

'Should we ask John and Fay to join us,' Amanda suggested. 'Then we could have a larger boat.'

'That'd be great' John, his godfather, had assumed glamour in Simon's eyes when he went abroad to work. On his leaves they had always done something exciting together, like camping. He had wondered what sort of a difference Fay would make. He grinned at his mother.

'I'll ask them. Then all we have to decide is which canal we choose,' said Amanda. 'Any preferences?'

From the beginning, Joe had never been mean with money and Amanda had wanted for nothing. She'd only had to ask. But when Simon started school Amanda decided the time had come for her to work to give herself an identity, discovering that it wasn't enough to be just Joe's wife or the mother of a son. Her five GCEs had got her into the local technical college but what Amanda had failed to do was to acquire any other qualifications since she had left so suddenly. She considered her options and concluded dolefully that she had none. Joe was opposed to her working, making it clear that he expected her to be home for Simon before and after school. That ruled out becoming a shop assistant again. In fact it ruled out most things.

It was Simon's teacher who provided the immediate answer. Would Mrs Williams consider giving an hour or so a week to hear some of the pupils read?

Amanda said she'd think about it. Secretly she was thrilled. No one had ever before assumed that she was capable of doing something essentially worthwhile. A little reluctantly she told Joe, believing that he would find all sorts of reasons why she should decline the offer.

'Do you get paid?' was the only thing he asked.

'No. No, I don't think money comes into it.'

'Then that means you can give it up the more easily. I don't suppose you'll find it very interesting for long because they're bound to give you the slow learners.'

He was wrong about that. She had no experience, then, with the slow learners. He was wrong about the other thing, too. She enjoyed the whole business of getting to the school before the lesson started, finding the books, collecting her little group, discovering how much they had read since she last saw them, whether they'd understood what they'd read.

'You have a natural talent for this, Mrs Williams,' said the class teacher warmly. 'Would there be any chance that you'd give us some more time? You see, Mrs Price has to finish in a week or so for the new baby.'

In the fullness of time Simon left primary school for the comprehensive. Amanda stayed on. So slowly that she hardly noticed, her hours were increased. To the reading she added little jobs like putting up the children's work on the classroom walls, staging their projects — she was good at that, too. On occasions she even began helping with their maths. After a few years a new head teacher was appointed. Amanda was invited to meet her officially.

It was a formal interview. For the first horrified few minutes, Amanda was convinced she was being asked to leave.

'You see, we have been given funds to appoint a Special

Teacher Assistant. It's virtually the job you've been doing for some time. I think you should apply for it.'

'But I haven't any qualifications.'

'I think you will find you have all that is necessary.'

The proper process had to be followed. The post was advertised; there was an interview. Amanda was appointed. Reeling, she told Simon.

'What'll Dad say?' was his reaction. 'Does he have to know?' he added pragmatically.

'He leaves so early on Mondays it hardly matters, and I'll be home on Thursday before he gets back. I can explain that I'm needed on Fridays as usual.'

That was how the matter stood. As for Amanda's salary, she banked almost all of it. She used some for clothes for the job. She bought petrol for her car. She paid for some of the outings Simon went on, treats that she felt it was too much to ask Joe to pay for. She kept the rest for emergencies. Just such a one was the proposed canal holiday.

Chapter Five

Sara

Henry Moody arrived a few days before the canal holiday, full of enthusiasm for their enterprise.

'Don't suppose narrow-boat engines are all that different from any other,' he said, so confidently that Sara felt the weight of dreadful anticipation lift from her.

Sara had continued to try to make Joe see sense about the holiday, as she thought of it, but it had been no use.

'It'll be great,' he insisted. 'We don't want to become one of those families that never attempts anything different, do we? Think of the children.'

'Of course not, and I am thinking of the children.'

Her caution had made him all the more determined. 'You wait and see.'

Her father's lack of concern was comforting. 'Remember those caravan holidays we used to take when you were young, love? Once you got accustomed to the way the park was run there was no problem.'

She allowed herself to be convinced.

Joe, Sara and their family picked up the *Meadow Sprite* at Great Hayward in the early afternoon. The narrow-boat, at sixty-five feet, loomed long and unwieldy to Sara's eyes as she lay moored in the suitably picturesque boatyard, but Sara's experience of boats in general went no further than pedaloes on a boating lake.

'I'll send the boy to take you through the first lock,' a voice said over her shoulder. Sara, her confidence once more at rock-bottom, mustered a sick smile for the boatyard owner, solid and cheerful, who then turned his attention to the ebullient Joe.

'Mummy, come and see. Come and see,' chanted the children, enthralled by what they had found.

Sara swallowed her panic, crossed the gangplank and descended into the bowels of what was to be their dwelling-place for the next week. A wave of relief swept over her as she realized the floor was steady under her feet. The interior was not unlike a caravan, but more spacious, solid, its fittings almost luxurious. She closed her eyes, swallowed again, opened her eyes and smiled weakly at her children.

'All right,' she said. 'Show me.'

The *Meadow Sprite* was semi-traditional in style and traditionally painted in black, red and green which delighted her. The rear deck was protected by solid sides, allowing little weather protection for the steerer but space for several people to sit on lockers. Forward was another deck with seating and a long passageway connected the two sets of stairs. There were two sleeping-cabins, both panelled in dark wood, one a double, the other with two bunk-beds, a vanitory unit and cupboards. The sitting-area would be converted into another double bed – hers and Joe's, Sara guessed, to allow David to get to sleep at a reasonable time. There was a TV – which she hoped they would not need to use – a shower and a separate lavatory (with a proper flush), a good-sized kitchen with an electric stove and fridge, all beautifully equipped down to a new packet of disposable cloths. She was most impressed.

David burst in. 'Port is right and left is starboard, isn't it, Mum?'

' 'Tarboard, 'tarboard, port and 'tarboard,' sang Nicola. 'Port and 'tarboard, Daddy, port and 'tarboard.' She skipped off to find her father.

Sara smiled. 'I think we'd better start unpacking the car, don't you.'

They had a Friday departure. Most of the boats turned round on a Saturday so the yard was very quiet. They spent an hour or so unpacking clothes and groceries and stowing away gear before returning their bags to the car. Harriet bought some postcards and Joe selected a large-scale map of their route.

The boatman's boy, a youth of about seventeen with an incipient growth of hair on his chin, came on board.

'New to this, then, are you?' he commented knowingly. Sara nodded, trying to swallow the lump in her throat that wouldn't quite melt. 'Which way do you want to go?'

'North along the Trent and Mersey.'

'Right you are.' The youth sent David ashore to cast off.

Sara looked apprehensive as she watched her small son coping – very efficiently – with the rope.

'Main thing is to have no passengers,' the youth said cheerfully. 'Can you swim?' he asked David, back on board. David shook his head. 'Better get your life jacket on, then,' he advised, but it was Harriet he was looking at now, with bold admiration as he took in the girl's tiny denim shorts, skimpy T-shirt, dangly earrings and long, bare legs. Harriet preened, her sulky look less obvious.

The boatyard was at the junction of the Staffordshire and Worcestershire canal with the Trent and Mersey, which involves an immediate, and sharp, turn directly under a small humpbacked bridge.

'Bit of a tricky one, that,' the youth pointed out unnecessarily as they scraped through, bringing his attention, reluctantly, back to the matter in hand. Joe grinned, Harriet looked startled. Sara was terrified.

Half a mile upstream they came to their first lock.

'You need a bit of weight for the paddles,' the youth observed. He glanced at Sara. 'You going to steer, then?'

'Ri-ight,' answered Joe for her, appearing a bit unwilling, for the first time. He got off the boat, jumping for the towpath.

'You'll need the windlasses.'

'Right.'

Each windlass operated a paddle which controlled the flow of water, thus enabling the two lock gates to be opened and closed. The paddles were stiff. Too stiff for Harriet so her grandfather had to help her.

'You'll get the hang of it very soon.'

The youth was definitely used to first-timers. He returned to Sara.

'Yours is the easy part. All you have to remember is not to get caught on the cill going downstream.'

He might have been talking Greek, she thought grimly, wondering if they would ever get that far.

The youth waited until the *Meadow Sprite* rose to the upper level, then he jumped off.

'See you in a week, then,' he called cheerfully, and strode away with a special smile and a wave to Harriet, who looked even more gratified.

Joe and Sara regarded each other wordlessly.

'The next lock's not far off,' Joe said eventually. 'Let's get through that, then moor.'

Sara remembered Nicola. But she was in the forward cockpit, life jacket slightly askew, giving tea to her favourite doll under the watchfully caring eye of her grandfather. Sara began to relax.

There were no visible witnesses to their chequered progress through Weston Lock, unaided this time. Sara entered it at an angle and never felt fully in control. By the time they had found a suitable mooring it was after six, clouds had obscured the sun and it was getting chilly.

Thank heaven for central heating, thought Sara, as she prepared soup and scrambled egg. They were all thoroughly exhausted.

'The important thing is to remember this is a holiday,' Joe said. He appeared to sense that all was not quite as it usually was on the first evening of a summer holiday. He opened a bottle of white wine. 'It's going to be flat and industrial until we're past Stoke-on-Trent, but we'll go quietly and get a good meal somewhere in the middle of the day.'

'Fish 'n chips,' said David.

'What else?' agreed his father. 'For seafarers.'

'Freshwater idiots,' said his mother.

'Water idiots, water idiots . . .' Henry put a restraining arm round his smaller granddaughter.

'Well, I like the sound of that,' said Sara, looking at her wine with distaste. 'I think I'd have preferred a gin and tonic.' An expression of dismay crossed her face briefly. She got up. 'I think I'll just have a glass of water tonight.'

Joe looked a bit startled. 'I'd better make sure we get in sufficient tonics tomorrow.'

'Why not? As long as we remember to buy bread,' Sara added inconsequentially, unable entirely to forget the practicalities of self-catering, even in the anticipation of future family trauma.

Joe, Henry and Harriet went for a walk while Sara put the little ones to bed. They were very tired by the excitement and fell asleep immediately. Then the rest of them played rummy until Joe decided it was time to assemble the double bed.

Later still, as he settled Sara into the crook of his arm, he kissed and fondled her.

'It's going to be a great holiday, you wait and see.'

Drowsy from everything and the warmth of his arms, she murmured: 'Mm,' and kissed his ear. 'Sleep well,' she said, and fell deeply asleep.

Predictably there was a steady drizzle when they woke, but by the time they had breakfasted and cleared away the dishes the rain had more or less stopped. They chugged through six locks and then found a boatyard where they moored. Henry, ever practical, reminded them to take on water when it was available.

'I mentioned water to the boy. He said it often isn't available when you need it most.' Then they went to look for somewhere to eat.

They found a fish bar not far from the canal.

'Fish 'n chips,' said David eagerly.

'Mussels for me,' said Joe. 'Now that's a good old English dish.'

'Ugh. I want plaice,' said Harriet.

'And me, please,' said Sara. 'And on your own head be it if there's garlic in those mussels, Joe.'

They managed another four locks that day, Joe insisting that they continue until they reached the Wedgwood pottery where, according to their map, there was an interesting mooring not far from the visitor centre. Gazing around at the flat Midlands landscape, a depressed Sara hoped he was right. It was like a sepia print; the water of the canal, the sky, a few rusty iron girders, brick, some of it crumbling, the dun-coloured vegetation of the canal bank, even the clothes of a solitary fisherman, it seemed to her that all melded into a muddy monochrome. She made tea in a large pot with flowers on it and tried not to long too much for the sizzling colours of the Mediterranean of the previous year.

'It'll get better, you'll see,' Joe said confidently, as if he saw in her face what she was thinking.

After a cold supper, Henry put the children to bed while the other three went off to find a pub. Joe ordered a large whisky.

'Think I've overdone it today,' he said. 'Or caught a chill, or something. This'll settle me.' He was not very communicative, though, so after a couple of drinks they walked slowly back to their narrow-boat.

Just after midnight Sara woke suddenly. She thought at first it was one of the children, but an ashen-faced Joe staggered back to bed and collapsed, groaning. For the next few hours he was very ill and became flushed and feverish, shivering constantly.

'S-sorry,' he shuddered. 'Damn-fool thing to do. Shouldn't have touched those mussels. Must've been a bad one in the batch. Better stay here tomorrow.'

'Shell-fish poisoning?' Amanda diagnosed in panic. 'Oh, no, Joe.'

'No need to panic. I think I'll probably live.' He grimaced.

'Should we get you a doctor? What a good thing no one else ate the same dish,' she could not help adding.

'Let's wait until morning, shall we?'

In the morning Joe was no better. They transferred him to the double cabin so that they could use the table, and piled quilts on him to keep him warm. They used Joe's mobile to phone the boatyard for an NHS help number, and then persuaded the duty doctor to arrange for a prescription to be left out for Sara at a local chemist who, fortunately, opened for an hour on a Sunday morning. It took her well over three hours to find it, collect the medicine and walk back to the *Meadow Sprite*.

Harriet plied her with much-needed coffee and a sandwich, and then they debated whether it would not be better to abandon the holiday altogether, ask their boatyard to fetch them and return home with Joe.

'We could be back by this evening,' Sara pointed out, sensibly.

'Oh, Mum,' Harriet protested. 'I mean, well, you know I don't want to be unfair to Dad, but . . .'

'I should think Joe would be more comfortable if you left him until tomorrow,' said Henry. 'By then, the medicine'll probably be working and he'll be feeling capable of making decisions like that.'

'Yes, Dad,' agreed Sara slowly. She had also had one example of how difficult it was to obtain the simplest service on a Sunday. 'It would be a lot easier to wait until tomorrow. I'll see what Joe says.'

Joe was asleep.

'We'll wait until tomorrow,' Sara decided. At least it was fine.

The children played in the field behind the towpath. There was plenty to keep them happy, even just watching the boats go through the next lock which was only a little way upstream. Harriet made a fishing-rod for David from a stick and a bent pin and for ages he pretended to be a real fisherman. Yes, thought Sara, settling back with a novel, they would do very well where they were until morning.

Joe's diarrhoea and vomiting were controlled dramatically by the medicine and he spent most of the Monday sleeping. Sara had been warned that he would need a day or so to recover, which would play havoc with their schedule, but as the sun was still shining it was agreed that they would stay where they were for another couple of days then cruise slowly back to their base.

In the afternoon another boat from their yard moored nearby. A man and a woman wandered off hand in hand and two others, a young man and probably his mother, sat on the bank drinking tea. David and his fishing-rod edged nearer and nearer and eventually they began holding a conversation as to the relative merits of their respective boats. After ten minutes David came back to Sara, full of importance.

'Simon's Mum says may I stay and have a biscuit and some coke, and can I bring Nicola and Harriet, too? I told her Dad was sick.'

'That's kind of them,' replied Sara, who was washing out a pair of Joe's pyjamas. 'I'll have a cup of tea with your grandfather and come and fetch you in half an hour.'

The *Meadow Skylark* was the *Meadow Sprite*'s sister boat. Sara
thought, enviously, how much easier it must be to have two men
to cope with the locking, then she felt disloyal for, despite Joe's
sudden illness, she was actually beginning to enjoy herself. A
part of her realized that this was because they were not moving
and the only problems she had to face were those that involved
the family. Nevertheless, she did wonder what it would be like,
cruising gently along the canal, gazing idly at the drifting
scenery with nothing else to concern her and nothing to do.

Emerging from the other boat was a woman. The two eyed
each other and decided they liked what they saw, exchanging
pleasantries, commiserating over the sick husband.

'My husband is a Joe, too. He's in London.' In the manner of
holiday acquaintances, they did not exchange surnames. You
didn't, just in case the relationship proved a catastrophe.

'Mum. Simon asked me to go out with them this evening.'
Harriet was sparkling and she looked very pretty. Sara experienced sudden dismay. To her mind and not for the first time,
her elder daughter suddenly seemed a young woman when
really she was still only a child.

'That's nice, dear,' said Sara cautiously.

'We're going to find a pub,' Simon's mother, Amanda, told
her. 'Harriet's very young, isn't she. We'd take good care of her.'

'That's kind of you. After supper, then. She'll be a bit bored
if we have to stay here another day while her father recovers,'
Sara confided.

Sara saw them off, the five of them, the woman and her son,
one on either side of Harriet, Amanda's brother and his wife.
They seemed nice people. She felt sure Harriet would be quite
safe with them.

She was already in the reassembled double bed, reading by
a shaded light so as not to disturb Joe, when Harriet returned.

She did not sense the nervous excitement in her daughter's manner, nor see the almost hectic flush on Harriet's cheeks as the girl put her head round the door to say good-night.

'Had a good time, dear?'

'Great, Mum. Good-night.'

By breakfast-time Joe had graduated to weak tea but it was quite obvious he would not be able to handle the boat for another day at least. Sara was relieved, though she could see disappointment in the faces of her father and Harriet.

'We'll go and have a look round the pottery this afternoon,' she suggested brightly. Harriet gave her an indifferent shrug.

'That's a good idea,' encouraged Henry. 'The little ones and I will have a ball-game this morning.'

'What happens if the ball goes into the canal, Granddad? Can I jump in and fetch it?'

'Me. Me jump in,' said Nicola.

'Certainly not,' said Sara severely. 'Have you seen the state of the water? No one's jumping in. You'll just have to make sure you don't lose the ball.' An altercation was threatening when they were hailed from the bank.

Sara and Harriet went to investigate. It was Simon and John.

'We've come to make a proposition. We got the feeling last night that you were getting restless, just moored here.'

'I wouldn't say that,' Sara demurred.

'Mum. Simon's right. It is boring, just staying here. There's nothing to do at all.'

'So how would you like us to take over your boat and bring you with us through the Harecastle Tunnel and up into the Macclesfield Canal?'

'Oh, Mum! That'd be cool.'

Sara hesitated. All kinds of objections ran through her mind. Safety, well, safety first and last.

'It is kind of you. But not really a good idea, I think. You see, we'd have to come all that way back on our own and we've only got until Friday. Besides. . . . And I don't think my husband ought to do as much as that and I've heard that the Harecastle Tunnel is dreadfully hard work.'

'That's all right, Sara,' said Simon confidently. 'I didn't explain it properly. Actually, you'd be doing us a bit of a favour. I'm sure you understand that there really isn't much for me to do with Mum and John and Fay in our boat and we could easily do the locks in convoy. Then you'd see more of the scenery.' It was as if he had known all along exactly what she had day-dreamed about: lazily looking at the scenery while someone else did the hard work.

'Simon forgot to mention, again, that we'd make sure you were back at the yard by Friday,' John added. 'We'd spend our last day going further south. So it really wouldn't be putting us out, you see.'

'Go on, Mum. Say yes,' Harriet pleaded. 'It would be fantastic.'

It did have its points, Sara conceded. Especially for the children. But she didn't really want the responsibility of such a decision.

'I'll go and have a word with Joe.'

Joe was asleep.

'Why not?' Henry said when he was consulted. 'The children would love the extra company, you can see that. You could do with a bit of a rest, and Joe isn't likely to complain, is he?'

'Well, no. Not if we're back on time,' Sara agreed, still very unwilling. There was something . . . She couldn't quite put her finger on it. 'And they do seem nice people,' she said, more warmly than she intended. Was it Harriet? The proximity of a very good-looking boy? She could always keep a close eye on her daughter. It was too bad of her to foster unwarranted suspicions.

'All right, then,' she decided. 'I suppose I'd better tell them to cast off. It's lucky I gave Joe some sweet tea an hour ago. I don't think he'll want anything more for some time.'

Round midday Davey clambered on to the roof where Sara was sunbathing.

'Hey, you,' she said, 'I thought we agreed you wouldn't do any climbing while we were on the move.' She couldn't bring herself to sound too cross for he was looking so assured.

'It's Dad. We heard him calling and Granddad sent me to find out what he wanted.'

'Is he all right?' Sara sat up in alarm.

'He's fine, Mum. Well, I suppose he isn't, because he said he's thirsty.'

'Thanks, love. I didn't hear a thing. I'll take him some orange-juice.'

'I'm very thirsty,' Joe complained, as Sara entered carrying a large glass.

'I'm sorry, love. I thought you were sleeping. It's a lovely day and I've been on the roof, sunbathing.'

There was a certain amount of shouting, then the note of the engine changed. After that there was a slight bump, and silence.

'What's going on? Why're we moving?' Joe asked petulantly.

'I'm not surprised you're ready for this,' Sara said, not quite prepared for all the explanations that would follow. She propped him up with an extra pillow then handed him the frosted glass. 'How are you feeling now?'

'Thirsty. Terrible. Well, a little better, I suppose.' He grinned sheepishly.

'Any thoughts about having something to eat? I could do you some toast or even something more substantial.' There was another thump and the *Meadow Sprite* rocked. Joe spluttered over the orange juice.

'What's been going on?' he demanded, when she had taken the glass and wiped the outside before handing it back. 'Are we back at Great Hayward?'

Of course, he would have assumed that she had organized the boatyard to come and fetch them. That was why he had not been too perturbed when he realized they were moving. She began to explain. At first Joe was aghast, ready to leap out of bed and confront the interlopers.

'You mean to say you just let a party of strangers take over our boat?' he spluttered. 'Just like that! What about the insurance, Sara, did you think about that?'

'Hang on,' she protested. 'They may be strangers, but we all like them a lot. There are four of them. Simon, who has just left school, is helping Dad take us through a few locks. The rest of their family are on their own boat. It was all right for David and Nicola. They wouldn't mind where we were for the novelty of it all, but it was a bit boring for Harriet, you know, stuck where we were,' and she tried not to sound reproachful for it certainly wasn't Joe's fault that he'd got food-poisoning.

Then she explained the bit about the boy and his uncle wanting something more to do; about their promise to have the *Meadow Sprite* back at the boatyard by Friday.

'The little ones are so thrilled,' she told him. 'They're all having lunch in their own boat now but I'll bring one of them in to see you before we cast off, if you like.'

'Looking as if I've been at death's door!' he expostulated. 'Heavens, no. If they are what you say, I'll lie back for today and let them get on with it. Maybe tomorrow I'll shave and emerge, pale and interesting.'

'That sounds as though you've turned the corner, love,' said Sara, and laughed indulgently. 'And they truly are what I said, Joe. Really nice. If it's another fine day tomorrow it'd be good for you to sit out in the sun and watch the world drift by. And now, what about that toast?'

Joe closed his eyes. 'If you like,' he said, a patient once more.

Sara stretched across and kissed his bristly cheek.

'Go back to sleep, love. I'll be back with the toast in a minute. Then if there's anything more you want, all you have to do is call.'

Chapter Six

Joe on Joe

Sara loved treacle tart, too, though mostly I bought her fruit-cake.

You remember that each Thursday I gave Amanda a treacle tart which purportedly came from Aunt Ethel? On Monday morning I handed over a fruitcake to Sara. That was also a standing order from the WI stall. I bought food containers which I kept in the boot so that neither the tart nor the cake would get spoiled. I liked an occasional bit of fruitcake with my mid-morning coffee and it kept for the weekend when Sara and the children enjoyed it. She said she was very pleased that Aunt Ethel thought to give her something she would otherwise have had to find time to bake – or buy a cake containing E-thingies from the supermarket.

A cynic might say that if I hadn't met Sara I would have found someone else, that I was ready for the next adventure when she appeared. It's not true, for as I said before no one sets out to complicate his life unnecessarily. What happened with Sara came about purely because of who she is.

I told you that once Aunt Ethel died and I installed a house-keeper in her house I had plenty of spare time. Of course there was always paperwork which filled some evenings but there were many hours when I was at a loose end. I didn't much care for TV and those were the days when the film business was in the doldrums. Sometimes I went to classical concerts but what I did enjoy was walking. I mean real walking, not just strolling round town. I didn't join a club or anything because I'm not a club person.

Instead, a couple of nights a week I'd take myself into the countryside to stretch my legs, even in the winter or when the weather was bad, though I was never foolhardy enough to go high on those occasions.

There was this evening when I'd finished the paperwork sooner than I'd expected. It was too late to go out of town so, as it was a beautiful evening, I thought I'd do a couple of circuits in the park. (Walking, not jogging; I have too much respect for my bony skeleton for that activity.) She was there, sitting on a bench, examining the high heel of her shoe which had broken. She was still there when I passed the second time. I mean to say, damsel in distress, knight in shining armour; for goodness sake, what was I supposed to do?

There really is no need to go into the finer points of what happened next. Sara just sat there and allowed me to take over, and I was happy to do it. She looked at me with her pain-filled eyes and I felt as though I was drowning. It struck me almost immediately that she reminded me of someone – though it wasn't until the next day that I realized how closely she resembled Amanda. I guess I must have been feeling pretty lonely that night. Of course, it helped that Sara was pretty and grateful, though I like to think I would have done the same if she had been elderly and/or crippled. I gave her my arm and supported her while we hobbled out of the park to my car – she'd also turned her ankle painfully. I drove her home. She hardly spoke until we arrived at her house, an unremarkable detached property – though in a good part of town. It could have ended there, only she wanted me to go in for a cup of coffee. She lived with her parents, she said. Suddenly she didn't seem to want me to go, but I couldn't be doing that, now could I?

So Sara suggested we might meet for a drink. 'My ankle'll be so much better by tomorrow,' she insisted.

And I agreed.

It should have ended there, only one thing led to another and before I knew it we were dating regularly and suddenly I had no free time. There came a moment when I had to explain to her why I could never see her at the weekend. She was having a small party for her eighteenth birthday and wanted me to be there. What could I say: that I was married, that I spent Thursday to Monday with my wife? Come on, would you have confessed?

I told her about Aunt Ethel. I explained that the old lady needed me to manage her factory, that on condition I kept the place going I would inherit. I told her how demanding Aunt Ethel was and how there was no chance things would change for many years. Sara was furious and stormed out of the wine bar, vowing we were finished.

Why didn't I take her at her word? Because I was already more than half in love with her. She was adorable, good company to be with, drove me well-nigh crazy with her kisses (she was a virgin and in those days not all young people leaped into bed at the first opportunity). Several weeks later we met, by chance (was it?) in our favourite wine-bar. I honestly don't remember who made the first move, but by the end of the evening the quarrel was over.

It was then that I made my second big mistake. I suggested we should go away together for a few days. She was shocked and refused. I wasn't really surprised. In fact, I think I would have been dismayed if she had agreed. Nice girls didn't do things like that, in those days. But, being me, I couldn't leave things there. It was obvious that she wanted commitment (marriage?) and I needed to reassure her that she meant something to me.

'I don't just want to take you to bed. Well, of course I do, but I want to spend time with you. It's not easy here.'

'I thought — I thought you were coming to love me.'

'I am. I do.'

Poor love. Was I trying to scare Sara away? I don't know. I knew I could not betray Amanda, cause her more suffering than I had already. Legally I was free to marry but, still loving Amanda, I was morally bound to her in a way that was stronger than any man-made law. (Also, in the back of my mind was the knowledge that the fewer lies I told the better.)

'Whatever my feelings are for you, you have to know that marriage scares me, that I have seen too many loveless marriages and I am not prepared to let it happen to me.'

'I love you, Joe,' she said then. 'And I always will.'

I knew she meant it and I was becoming more smitten by her by the day.

There was one other thing, her parents. I'd met them by that time, though only a couple of times. I'm not sure that Mrs Moody ever really approved of me. She always looked at me as though she was sure there was something wrong with me and that one day she would discover what it was. (She died before Henry and at least that never happened.) The very suggestion that her daughter might consider living in sin would have affronted her, and Sara was well aware of it.

I imagined that would be the end of marriage hopes, whatever it did for our relationship. I underestimated my lovely Sara. A week or so later she suggested that we just lived together; that she became my common-law wife. I was amazed she even knew what that meant.

What would you have done? I expressed disbelief, abhorrence. It was so stupid to take the moral high ground then and Sara saw through me and my protestations. She was quietly adamant — which flabbergasted me, frankly, because I think I'd thought of her previously as being a little immature. In the end, though, I realized that this was the perfect solution. We had another serious talk. As far as possible I needed her to understand what her situation would be. I returned to the question of Aunt Ethel. I said that I wasn't prepared to abandon the old lady, that if Sara accepted that we could only be together for half of the week, from Monday to Thursday, we could set up home together.

Sara agreed immediately. Maybe she hoped that one day I would change my mind. Maybe that was why she went along with all my suggestions, including where we would live. This led me to problem number two, the one I could not disclose, the sheer complexity of managing two factories miles apart as well as two households. There was a possibility of enlarging the Cwmbran plant by acquiring land next to it that was coming on to the market. I'd had advance notice from the owner and I'd already toyed with the idea of acquiring it but I'd had to abandon it regretfully for lack of funds. Now, if I sold the Midlands plant the money would be available. As luck would have it, there was a ready buyer there, a man who had cash to spare for an investment and who didn't particularly want it to be known that the plant had changed hands.

Naturally it all took time because I also had to find a house on the other side of Cwmbran. Having the two households in the same area made the same sense as enlarging the Cwmbran works. I just had to trust that there would be little prospect of the two women meeting. Well, man proposes . . . I know that. It was going to be a risk I had to take.

So, as far as Sara was concerned, because of the works she and I lived in Cwmbran and I visited Aunt Ethel each weekend, overseeing the Midlands plant every Friday.

When it came to the actual ceremony – or lack of one – it was Sara who suggested we should stage an elopement, pretending that we both hated the prospect of a large wedding. We flew to Antigua and, with the help of a handout or three to some obliging bystanders, staged photographs of the happy couple. It really wasn't that difficult.

Interestingly, once we had returned home, Sara's parents accepted me, if not entirely with open arms, at least as though I was their legal son-in-law. It no doubt helped that Sara became pregnant with Harriet very quickly and that Henry was left a widower not long afterwards. The advent of David was an amazing thing – we'd both given up all thoughts of a second child.

You may be wondering if I had the same feelings of panic about Harriet, David and Nicola, as I'd had with Simon? I was actually waiting for the panic attack, which never came. I don't understand why it was different this time. Maybe it was because I'd learnt that babies didn't break, that you didn't drop them if you were careful. Perhaps I'd also learnt to take the emotional side as it came.

There was also the fact that after a few days with Harriet I left her with Sara and returned to the more robust small boy, and once the novelty of my engaging son had begun to wear off, I went back to my cute and lovable little daughter, who is developing into a drop-dead gorgeous, if pouty teenager, and has been joined by her serious and undoubtedly brilliant brother and my little Nicola who causes my heart to turn over afresh each time I see her.

I don't suppose I deserve that the *status quo* should have continued any longer. I accept that what happened next has to be my fault.

Chapter Seven

Amanda

The *Meadow Sprite* and the *Meadow Skylark* joined the line of ten other craft moored at the mouth of the Harecastle Tunnel, at 2897 yards the longest and most difficult to navigate of all the canal tunnels.

'Have you decided how we do this?' Amanda asked Simon and her brother who were with her on the lead boat, conferring in the sun.

'I'm going to steer the *Skylark*,' said John, 'I think young David wants to come to our boat so I thought you, Fay and he could go forward to guide us through the unlit sections.'

'Sounds fine by me. What will you do, Simon?'

'I'm steering the *Sprite*. Harriet and Sara will guide us.'

'The first boat is casting off.' David scrambled on board. 'Mum wants to know what to do.'

'We're coming,' answered Simon, and he jumped on to the towpath. 'See you the other end. Ready to cast off yourself, John?'

'Be careful,' called Amanda from force of habit. Simon waved, managing to put a heavy degree of irony in the gesture. She sighed. 'I suppose one day I'll learn.'

'What's that?' John asked, catching the painter.

'Simon. You know. To think before I speak.'

'My dad says he always thinks first,' said David.

'Good for your dad,' said John. 'Now, David, suppose you stow the rope neatly.'

'The painter?'

John grinned. 'That's right. D'you want to stay with me or go forward with Amanda?'

'May I stay here?'

'Sure. Ready, Amanda?'

'Going right away. What've you done with Nicola?' she asked David over her shoulder as she climbed on to the narrow-boat's roof, which at first she had found scary, though it was quicker than going through the boat.

'She's with Granddad in the saloon. Just like a girl, she says she doesn't think she'll like the dark.'

'I expect it will seem a bit creepy because it's so long.'

Whatever effect the eerie, damp darkness had on Nicola, it upset Fay, who seemed incapable of fending the narrow-boat away from the old towpath that still existed in parts of the tunnel. Every so often there was a gentle scrape and a shout of protest from John at the other end, the sound bouncing boomingly off the old, crumbling brickwork. It was difficult to imagine men guiding the horses that had pulled the old narrow-boats, their holds filled to the brim with all manner of goods in the heyday of the industrial Midlands. Fleetingly Amanda wondered about accidents that had happened to them, shuddered and went back to concentrating on keeping their boat straight. Later, Amanda looked across at Fay, whose eyes were glittering in the gleaming light from their headlight, which illuminated the curved roof of the tunnel. Should she send her back to John? If she did, the work of fending off would be even more difficult.

'I really don't like this,' said Fay, her teeth clenched, reinforcing Amanda's fears.

'It can't be far now. Or would you rather go back to John?'

'I'll manage.'

They worked in silence. After a long while there was a pinprick of light ahead, which gradually filled their horizon until they emerged into the sunlight once more.

'Sorry,' Fay said reluctantly.

'That's all right. I didn't realize you don't like the dark. Let's put the kettle on, or do you think it's time for a glass of wine?'

'I'll stick to tea.'

Amanda shrugged. 'I guess we'd better leave the wine for later.'

After the Harecastle Tunnel the canal bifurcates. The *Meadow Sprite*, and the *Meadow Skylark* took the left fork, swinging gently round to cross over the Trent and Mersey Canal where it becomes the quieter Macclesfield Canal. A further flight of six locks brought them to more open countryside where they had already decided to moor for the night. The air was cool, the scenery stark and magnificent. A lovely silence fell as the engines of both boats were cut and for a long moment no one stirred.

Then it was sound and movement as painters were tossed and caught, (dropped by Amanda and retrieved by David), pegs were hammered into the ground and the boats made secure for the night. Everyone was pleased with their progress.

'Today's been great,' Simon enthused when they all met up, and John and Henry agreed heartily.

Amanda and Sara, together for the first time that afternoon, smiled at each other, acknowledging tacitly that a holiday was so much more successful when the menfolk were happily engaged in something energetic. Amanda thought it was a pity that she and Fay had been paired off. It would have been more interesting to have spent the afternoon with Sara, though she realized that the other woman must have felt happier in her own boat with so many strangers around.

'We'll do the twelve Bosley locks tomorrow, then turn,' said John. 'If that's all right with everyone?'

'Excellent.' Simon beamed, casting a sidelong glance at Harriet.

'Twenty-four locks in one day,' exclaimed Sara. 'You must be joking.'

'Perhaps we could take just one boat through?' suggested John. 'Then anyone who wanted a quiet day could stay here.'

'That sounds fine by me,' said Amanda, who was looking at the darkish clouds massing on the horizon and thought she'd wait and see what the weather brought.

'And fine by me,' agreed Sara. 'I expect both Joe and I will stay here. And that reminds me. It's time for Joe's medicine.'

'Shall we see you all after supper?' asked John, as the crew of the *Meadow Sprite* gathered their things to return to their own boat.

'Mum?' asked Harriet, hovering by Simon, her eyes pleading. 'We thought we'd play card-games. Or Monopoly.'

'Please, Mum?'

'I don't . . .' began Sara cautiously. Then she relented. 'I suppose you can go along. If you aren't back too late.'

'We'll make sure she doesn't stay too long,' said Amanda. 'Sara, what about you?'

'Do go, dear,' said Henry. 'I'll stay behind with the little ones.'

'I can play Monopoly too,' said David indignantly. 'I'm much better than Harriet. She always buys the cheapest property and never seems to get any rent'

'David,' protested his mother, while Harriet gave her brother a furious nudge, then blushed as she realized she had been caught out behaving childishly. She tossed her head and the others smiled indulgently.

'Monopoly it is, and I guess David is invited, too,' said Amanda.

'I expect I shall have to wait and see how Joe is,' said Sara.

In the event, Joe decided he would prefer to watch some TV while he babysat his small daughter, so it was a noisy group, including Henry but not Sara or Amanda, who squeezed into the space round the saloon table to play Monopoly. The women retired aft where it was sheltered and where, wrapped in thick woollen sweaters, they sat in relative peace.

'Isn't it strange how we never mind sitting outside on holiday, whatever the temperature. I wouldn't dream of doing this at home,' observed Sara.

Amanda opened her mouth to ask where home was, then she thought better of it and merely commented:

'It has gone colder. Too cold for you?'

'Not a bit, and besides, it's quieter here.'

They both smiled as a gale of laughter filtered through the door. Amanda held out the bottle of wine but Sara shook her head.

'I'd prefer a glass of water, if you don't mind.'

'Sparkling or still?'

'Sparkling, if you have it, but tap water'll do fine. I'm a bit thirsty.'

Amanda came back with a large bottle of mineral water.

'I'm sorry your husband couldn't join us,' she said.

'Even if he had felt up to it, one of us would have to stay with Nicola. She wouldn't have liked to wake up to find no one there.'

'Of course not.' Amanda made a gesture of apology. 'You forget how it is when you have little ones.'

'What a coincidence, our husbands having the same name? Still, I don't expect you ever really forget how it was with a baby, however long ago it was. I am glad we met up.'

Amanda thought fleetingly how no one who had not experi-

77

enced it for themselves could guess just how difficult it had been for her in those years when Simon was so very dependent on her and there was no one else to cope but herself.

'It was tough. There were times when I thought I would go out of my mind.' Why had she told Sara that? Amanda had one or two close women friends but only those she'd known for many years were given more than an inkling of her private thoughts and feelings – and no one knew the real story about Michael and Joe. 'Don't get me wrong,' she added, seeing an emotion she was unable to interpret cross the other woman's face. 'I adore Simon. I did, even when he was so helpless and needed me so much and I was totally exhausted and couldn't imagine when it would end.'

'I am sure your Joe was a great comfort.'

'Yes. Though there were times when he was away on business.' How could she elaborate? It was true she had always had Joe's mental and financial support, even when he was not there physically.

'I suppose it's the way of the world nowadays for business-men to have to travel,' Sara commented. 'I'd hoped my Joe would have felt well enough for some company tonight. If he doesn't get any fresh air I'm afraid he'll not sleep.'

'And the beds really aren't big enough for threshing around, are they?'

They both smiled in a way that spoke volumes of every marriage where perfect middle-of-the-night harmony did not always reign.

'At least Joe doesn't snore . . .'

'Joe's never been a snorer . . .'

They spoke as one, stopped and giggled.

'I'm looking forward to meeting him,' said Amanda, wishing that her own Joe had not been so adamantly against a canal holiday. 'Joe wants to take us to Ibiza in late August. He could-n't get away now so I thought I'd bring Simon on my own.

Fortunately my brother and his wife decided to come too, so that's made such a difference. Though I suppose we were a bit extravagant, hiring such a large boat'

'And lucky you, with the locks. I don't think Joe – my Joe – had any idea what he was letting himself in for when he booked this. David is so keen, but he hasn't the weight to work the paddles. And I'm not sure that Harriet has the inclination. Simon is very active, isn't he.'

'He's mad about any sport. Cricket of course, currently. I hope he doesn't give it all up at university. But you know what they're like, anything for a change.'

'You're waiting for results also, are you? Harriet did her GCSEs this summer.' Harriet's mother sighed, 'I don't think we're going to be too pleased with our results, though.'

'Mm. Aren't children an endless problem? Simon says he'll be fine, but underneath it all you do wonder if it's bravado.'

'I think maybe we don't give the young enough credit for sense. After all, if the worst happens and his grades aren't what he expects, it's not the end of the world.'

For a while they discussed the merits of a university education in the manner of mothers worldwide.

'I didn't go to university, did you?' said Sara wistfully.

'No,' answered Amanda wryly. 'Then, I became pregnant too soon.'

'What do you do?' asked Sara.

Amanda was aware of . . . relief? Pleasure? She was not sure which predominated over Sara's assumption that she did have a career. That was what having an occupation outside the home did for you, gave you status.

'I'm a specialist teacher assistant.'

'That must be a worthwhile job.'

She had not called it either lucrative or interesting — though it was at least interesting. Once again Amanda warmed to this woman who had the knack of saying just the right thing to make you feel good about yourself.

'I drifted into it,' she admitted. 'Got cajoled into applying for the post, then discovered that with one year's part-time training I was sort of official. I really love the job. It's so rewarding when a child suddenly reads and you know that the whole world of books is waiting to be explored. In fact,' she hesitated, 'once Simon is settled I think I might do a degree myself, end up with a proper teaching qualification.' Now why hadn't she thought about that before? Well, she supposed she had, once or twice, but had dismissed it as being totally impractical. Besides, what would Joe say?

'How very brave of you. Would you go to the same college as Simon?'

'Heaven forbid,' said Amanda fervently. Sara smiled in the dark. 'It will probably have to be an Open University degree because I doubt if I could afford anything else.' It wasn't impossible, though, Joe or no Joe.

'Isn't that very hard work?'

'Yes. I expect it's just a pipe-dream.'

'I don't think you should call it that unless you really know it is an impossibility,' said Sara gravely.

'Thank you,' said Amanda, startled. 'You know, it isn't very often that I get taken seriously. I'll really think about it. So,' she changed the subject determinedly, 'what do you do, Sara?'

'I work from home. I do Joe's secretarial work. It does us very well, me being around for the children and Joe not having to employ anyone else.'

'I hope he pays you properly,' said Amanda 'Oops. Sorry. That sounded awful and definitely none of my business.'

'I don't get a wage,' Sara admitted slowly. 'Joe gives me a generous allowance for the family and if I need anything extra he never says no.'

'Ah.' There really didn't seem much more to say that wouldn't be considered unkind or intrusive.

'Though now I come to think about it, I'm not sure whether we wouldn't get more of a tax advantage if I was on the payroll. I wonder why I never thought about that before?'

Both were thinking, why had Joe never thought about that?

There was a pause. It was not uncomfortable. Amanda thought that it was a pity their acquaintance would last no more than to the end of the week. She would have enjoyed having Sara as a friend.

She was about to ask where Sara lived when there was another surge of noise. This time it was one of protest. Henry emerged, ushering in front of him a defiant David.

'It's time this young man was in bed. He's won the jackpot and won't sleep at all for the glory of his big head unless he goes now.'

'Granddad . . .'

'My goodness. Is that really the time. Come along, love. It's way past your bedtime.'

'I'll take him, dear.'

'Thanks, Dad. Amanda, I must collect Harriet. I'm sure we've long outstayed our welcome.'

'They've started another game. I don't think you'd be very popular.'

'You go, if you must,' said Amanda. 'I'll get Simon to bring Harriet back once the game is over.'

Sara seemed to go reluctantly. But Amanda, having enjoyed the evening very much, thought nothing of it and made hot chocolate. When the game was over she spoke to Simon.

'Escort Harriet home now,' she said.

'I can go on my own,' the girl answered quickly. Simon was already on his feet.

'Certainly not,' declared his mother. 'I know it isn't far but it's very dark. We wouldn't want you tripping over a mooring rope and falling into the canal.'

'Particularly as I'm a better swimmer than John and I'd be the one who had to dive in and rescue you.'

'Jump in,' said Harriet, giggling. 'The canal is too shallow for diving.'

'Got the torch, Mum,' said Simon, brandishing it.

'Good night, Harriet, then. See you in the morning.'

Amanda watched them cross the gangplank. The towpath was wide where they had moored, and it permitted them to walk side by side. Harriet was a pretty girl, Amanda thought. She'd probably be a real beauty when she had grown into her body. It was no wonder Simon was making a play for her attention. The torchlight became motionless. Amanda screwed her eyes up and focused on the snatched kiss.

'Escort duty only, I said,' she called, her voice low but penetrating.

There was a distinct sound of laughter. ' 'Night, Mum,' came back to her mockingly.

'I mean it.'

'Goodnight, Amanda.' That was Harriet. There was no hint that she would have preferred to be in the company of anyone other than the boy she was with.

Amanda shivered in the night breeze that had sprung up. It was the holidays, for goodness sake. They only had another hundred yards to go to the other boat. She trusted her son. Amanda shook her head at herself as she retreated into the warmth.

John and Fay had already cleared away the mugs, and were tidying the saloon.

'I'll leave the door for Simon to lock,' she said. 'I wouldn't be surprised if he doesn't go for a walk once he's seen Harriet to her boat. Don't bother to wait up. You've got work to do tomorrow.'

'Will you come with us?'

'I expect so. It'll be good just having time to read a book.

Though maybe I'll stay here and get to know Sara better. She's nice, isn't she.'

'Perhaps we'll get to meet her Joe tomorrow.'

'Maybe we will.'

Chapter Eight

Sara

Sara found Joe sitting at the table, coffee-mug in front of him, book in his hand, when she returned from the other boat.

'David's gone to bed, I hope,' she said, as she leaned over her husband to kiss his cheek.

He patted her behind. 'Went out like a light. I gather he's a property millionaire now.' He grinned. 'Henry was telling him he ought to think about becoming an estate agent when he's older.'

'Dad didn't.'

'Don't worry, Davey didn't think much of it, either. Said he's more likely to become a property tycoon.'

'I'm amazed he knows the meaning of the word.'

'He probably doesn't.'

'Nicola asleep?' Sara didn't bother to wait for the answer. Their daughter fell asleep more quickly than her brother, even if the downside was that she always woke first either to clamber into her mother's bed — when Joe wasn't there — or devise an elaborate game with her dolls. 'I'm glad to see you out of bed. You're looking so much better. How do you feel?'

'Better. I was hungry, too, so I made myself a couple of boiled eggs with bread and butter and I had a banana and now I'm having a cup of milky coffee. Where's Harriet?'

'She and the others are just finishing a final game, then Simon will bring her back. I don't suppose she'll be very long. I think I'll get in a shower first. Are you going back to bed or will you wait up for a bit?'

'I'll catch the news on the TV. I expect Harriet'll be back by then so I'll get to hear what's been going on.'

Sara went into the bathroom thinking how good it was to have Joe back to normal. It had been such a shame for him to be taken ill on the one week in the year when they were all together. She showered, brushed her teeth and creamed her face, eventually emerging clad in pyjamas a little later, to find the TV off and Joe drumming his fingers on the table top.

'What's the matter?'

'Harriet hasn't come back yet'

'Oh. She is late,' Sara frowned.

'I think I'd better go and fetch her.'

'Is that a good idea?'

'I could do with some fresh air and exercise before I go back to bed.'

'A hundred yards? Some exercise.'

Joe smiled. 'You know what I mean.'

'Actually,' Sara said slowly, thinking it through. 'I'm not sure it is such a good idea.'

'Fetching my daughter. Why ever not?'

'I don't mean that, exactly. She's used to you fetching her from choir practice, after all. But it is late and you've not met any of them. How would you like it if a strange man knocked at your door at this hour? You'd probably frighten the life out of Amanda.'

This time Joe frowned. Then he shook his head as if he knew there was something odd but thought it could wait.

'Well someone has to go,' he said. 'She knows she's not allowed out at this hour, even in the holidays.'

Sara saw the frown and was on the point of asking her husband if there was anything wrong. But Harriet's lateness was more important and besides, she had caught the expression of annoyance in Joe's voice.

'Why don't I put tracksuit bottoms on and come with you? I'll knock at the door and haul her out while you wait on the towpath and then we can both bring her back together.'

The first stars were pulsating overhead with only a few clouds drifting across the sky, so that the light from the orangey moon that was almost full was bright enough for them to be able to see the path without using the torch Joe had grabbed as they left the boat. Sara was thinking idly how lucky they were not to have the usual urban light pollution when they reached *Meadow Skylark*.

'The gangplank's still there so it doesn't look as though they've gone to bed. Just give me a minute, Joe.'

'I'll continue along the towpath for a bit.' He stretched. 'It's good to be out. I hate being cooped up.'

'No,' John, who answered her knock, said. 'They left about twenty minutes ago. Do you think they might have gone for a walk?'

'Why didn't I think of that? Sorry I bothered you. Good night.' Wretched girl, she was thinking. It was so thoughtless of Harriet not to have come back to *Meadow Sprite* immediately. She might have guessed her parents would worry. Especially since she was out with such a personable young man. *Anxious mother complex, again.*

'They think they might have gone for a walk,' she called, and waited for Joe to walk back to her.

'No matter,' said Joe easily. 'But I don't think they could have come this way. It's more likely they started off back to our boat, decided to prolong the evening and ambled along past us. I expect we just missed them.'

She noticed that the fresh air and the bit of a stroll had

soothed her husband's irritation. That was good.

'I expect you're right, dear. Let's go and find them. They can't be far away.'

An owl hooted. 'Listen to that,' he said. 'You don't hear that on a Mediterranean beach.'

He caught hold of her hand, swinging it companionably as they walked.

It was Joe, known for his acute hearing, who heard the voices first.

'It sounds as though someone's in that field,' he said, and fumbled for the torch. There was a large gap in the hedge which at that point was wide and straggly. The gap was closed by a decrepit wooden gate. Joe shone the torch into the field and focused it on the spot from where the voices seemed to be coming.

Sara, standing at the gate beside him, gazed in total incomprehension at the scene that was now illuminated.

'Harriet, no!' Harriet's father gave a strangled yelp, and banged his fist impotently on the top bar of the wooden gate.

In the torchlight the tableau froze. Then the girl struggled to a sitting position, throwing off the boy who made no attempt to escape but scrambled to his feet and stood there. Her eyes were wide with a fright that was apparent to her mother.

'Dad?' Harriet said uncertainly. She peered into the gloom behind the light. 'Dad. Is that you?'

'You little . . .' Joe grated and swung the torch to illuminate his own face. 'You'll know it's me before you're very much older, see if you don't!' Then he swung the torch back to the couple. Harriet was beginning to sob as she hitched her T-shirt back on to her shoulders covering her breasts. Beside her, the boy hung immobile.

Then he said: 'Dad? What are you doing here, Dad?'

Slowly the beam of light lit each face, one astonished, one

with tears running down it.

'What's happening?' Sara whispered. No, it was impossible, she was thinking, she could not have seen what she thought she had seen. 'Joe, what is this all about? What has Harriet been doing?' she asked stupidly, for she knew with absolute certainty exactly what her daughter had been doing and it was so momentous a thing that she was stupefied.

'Oh, God,' muttered Joe beside her, turned and lurched away into the darkness like a very old man.

For some reason Sara found herself unable to move. Disjointed thoughts flickered through her mind: *That's my daughter . . . But she's only sixteen . . . What does Harriet know about boys? . . . She knows what I told her . . . I warned her . . . Haven't I warned her? She knows there are things you do and . . .* Afterwards she could never explain why she did not immediately climb over the gate, grab Harriet and drag her back to the safety of their boat. Had Joe still been with her no doubt she would have expressed herself even more forcibly than Harriet's father. The thing was, Joe had left her.

Reason said that this was because he had witnessed something so sickening that it had thoroughly upset his already tender stomach. Joe had seen something so bad it had made him sick to the stomach? Sara shook her head to clear it, and for the moment, firmly setting aside the dubious morality of being a voyeur, she stayed where she was. Joe had also left her without the torch. Harriet continued to sob.

'Oh, do shut up, Harriet,' Sara heard Simon say at last, crossly. 'You haven't exactly been hurt by anyone, you know.'

'You don't, like, understand,' she hiccupped. 'I mean – that that was my father. He'll kill me,' she ended dramatically.

Sara stirred. It was quite likely she would do just that herself, she was thinking with rising anger, for Harriet had quite forgotten that Joe had never once raised his hand to her in anger.

'Your father, was it?' Simon said enigmatically. 'Well, well. I suppose we'd better be getting back, then. Oh, fuck, I've dropped the torch and I can't fucking find it.'

It was the language as he approached the gate and the prospect of being caught — as Joe had caught the two of them — that alerted Sara to the very real prospect of another confrontation. She shrank into the shadows of a conveniently overhanging elder. There was something very strange going on here and if she could she was determined to stay and attempt to find out what it was.

'Come on,' Simon said. 'We'll have to manage without the fucking thing.'

Harriet followed him, scrambling clumsily over the top bar. The moon had been obscured for a few minutes by a small cloud. Harriet stumbled just as she passed her mother and for a moment Sara was sure she had been discovered. 'Simon,' she heard Harriet say, in a peculiarly thin little voice. Simon stopped, his back uncompromisingly to her. 'You, like, called my father, "Dad". I mean, he's my dad, so . . .'

'I did, didn't I.'

'I don't understand,' said Harriet plaintively, echoing Sara's own chaotic thoughts. 'I mean, what're you getting at?'

'Your dad is mine, too,' Simon replied eventually. 'It appears. Somehow,' he added uncertainly.

In the shadows, Sara covered her mouth with her hand.

'You see, it seems that our father is a tiny bit upset because not only has his little secret come out, he found us just about to commit incest,' explained Simon, his voice exuding patience and reasonableness. 'At least, that's what could have happened. Unless you'd said "No,". Though I didn't get the impression you were resisting very hard. Interesting, that.'

Harriet was standing where she had stopped.

'Oh,' she said. Then she repeated the word. 'Incest? I – um. . . . Oh,' she said, again. After that she said, 'But that

89

means, like . . . I mean, if your father is my father, your mother—'

'Exactly,' agreed Simon.

There was a pause. 'I — um — don't usually go the whole way. At least . . .'

'Not the first time?'

Sara could have sworn she heard a hint of humour in his voice. She wasn't sure which was the more shocking, finding her daughter in this situation or the situation itself.

'What are we going to do?' Harriet asked.

'I'm not going to do anything, tonight,' Simon answered. 'Besides, I don't know about you, but I don't feel particularly guilty, so I intend sleeping with a clear conscience. I wasn't to know it was my sister I fancied, was I?'

'Nor me. My brother, I mean. But now we do, it must change things.'

'Everything's changed,' said Sara slowly, emerging from the shadows. It was bad enough that she had not let them know she was there sooner, she knew that. To allow Harriet to bear this . . . thing . . . unsupported would be a betrayal beyond anything the child's father might have done.

'Mum? I thought you'd gone back with Dad?' To her mother the change in Harriet's voice from uncertainty to accusation was plain. 'Did you hear all that?'

'Of course she did.'

Having announced her presence, Sara was incapable of taking the initiative immediately. It was moments before she said quietly:

'You are telling us that you are Joe's son?'

Simon shrugged. 'S'obvious, innit?'

'What's obvious? Mum, tell them it's not true. It can't be true,' Harriet wailed.

'Some people say I look like my father. I've always thought I was more like Mum. But you're right, it has all changed, like that twinkling of an eye business. I don't know why that should be. After all, we're still basically the same people. Me, Harriet. But it has. All the same . . .' and he kicked a stone viciously in the direction of the river, 'it's not exactly us who've got the explaining to do, is it? How do you think Dad'll explain Sara away to Mum, let alone Davey and Nicola. I suppose . . . ?' and he looked enquiringly at Sara, who nodded in the moonlight.

'They're his too,' said Harriet.

'Now there'a a thing.' Simon chuckled sardonically. 'Er, sorry, Sara.'

Sara's head was thick, her mind was a blank, her legs felt wooden.

'Time we were all in bed, if you ask me,' Simon said abruptly. 'Especially since we've got to do all those locks tomorrow.'

Could she hear compassion in his voice? How dared he. Sara's spine stiffened.

'Is that all you have to say?'

'I think we've all said quite enough for tonight, don't you?' As though he were her own son, Simon took hold of Sara's arm. Revolted by the boy's touch, the thought that this was no son of hers but a son of her husband by another woman, of whose existence she had not known until a few minutes before, she wanted to push him away, but she did not even have the strength to do that. Then she stumbled, her foot slipping into a shallow hole some nocturnal burrowing animal had started to dig. Simon kept firm hold of her until they reached the gangplank, supporting her on to the narrow-boat. After that he took Harriet's hand to help her, too, and when the two women were on board he walked away without another word.

Sara closed the door behind them and bolted it. *Closing the stable door?* She sighed. It was far too late for that, in every sense.

'Mum?' Harriet asked tentatively.

'Go to bed,' Sara answered wearily. 'We'll talk about it in the morning.'

'But Mum, I didn't . . . I mean . . .'

'I said, go to bed. It's far too late to talk about any of this now.'

'Is it really true that Dad . . . ?'

'Harriet, if you want to provoke me into losing my temper, you are going about it just the right way,' Sara said furiously. 'Now, go to bed and please don't wake Nicola.'

The evidence that her mother was at breaking-point seemed to have the desired effect. With what felt like tender compunction Harriet reached up and kissed Sara's cheek.

'I'm sorry, Mum,' she said penitently. 'Goodnight.' She hastened to bed.

Sara opened her mouth, about to yell that Harriet needn't think that that was any sort of an apology. Then she thought better of it. Finding her nubile daughter — for it occurred to her that that was exactly what she was: how slow she had been in recognising what was happening to Harriet — experimenting in the arms of a young man was relatively minor compared with discovering that Joe was the father of that young man.

She walked purposefully towards the dinette. As she passed the bathroom she could hear the sound of retching. So, Joe was sick to his stomach. A part of her rejoiced. She hoped someone had already put away the table and set up their bed. Of course no one had. They had left everything where it was to go and find Harriet. With rather more forcefulness than was absolutely necessary Sara put the dirty coffee-mug into the sink and put the kettle on for a cup of tea. While the tea was brewing she made up the double bed for the night, though she doubted she would get any sleep, certainly not if Joe was beside her. Joe. She sat on the bed with the tea in her hands.

What energy she had mustered over the past twenty minutes or so had quite vanished.

At last Joe emerged from the bathroom. He looked haggard.

'Joe. What has been going on?'

He gave a long sigh. Then he sat beside her on the bed. Instinctively she moved away. To hide it, for it felt unfair – unfair? — she offered him a cup of tea. He shook his head.

'Joe, what has been going on?' she repeated sharply. 'I don't mean just now. I mean, all of it, all these years?' The last word rose interrogatively.

He told her. It took time for he did not keep to a chronological sequence: 'This happened when?' she had to stop him, 'What happened then?' she made him tell her again.

There was a half-finished cup of tea on the chair beside her. Mechanically Sara reached out to pick it up. The rose-patterned cup rattled in its saucer. She put the china down as carefully as she was able. The tea would have been cold, anyway. She looked at Joe, surprised that she could look at him at all, let alone objectively. What did you say to a man who has been making you live a lie for, what was it? Nearly seventeen years. Recriminations. Accusations. She shook her head. He looked somehow pathetic, sitting there, hunched over his stomach as if the pain in it was too much to bear. Perhaps it was. Why? Why? Her brain agonized.

All those years she thought they had been happy. And yet he had never, in all that time, been satisfied with just her. The sense of her own obvious inadequacy made her burn with humiliation, though at the same time she seethed, her hand itching to fling the cold tea in his face. So much for imagining she was anything but passionately involved with this man.

Eventually she spoke.

'I don't believe it.' But, of course, she did, every word. 'That boy. You mean, Amanda ... but you said ... you said you didn't believe in marriage.'

'Simon is mine all right. Amanda and I are not married.'

'Why didn't you tell me the truth?' she asked bitterly.

Joe sagged. 'Would you have agreed to live with me if I had told you the truth, that there was someone else?'

'I don't know. Probably not. I would have done better if I had ditched you, wouldn't I?'

'Would you?' he countered softly.

'I don't know. Oh, how dare you make this out to be just a sexual thing. I loved you but if I had known you were involved with another woman, that there was a child. . . . I don't know.' Since Joe had never told her about Amanda, perhaps he had been courteous enough not to discuss his mistress with his wife. At least she and Amanda ought to get a laugh out of discussing Joe with each other. It was ironic that they liked each other so. The black humour of her thoughts almost made Sara smile. Almost, not quite.

'How could you!' she said bitterly, and added bitingly: 'At least I know now where Harriet gets her sexual morals from.' Joe glared at her as if he would have liked to offer her some sort of violence. He'd never done that before, either. Sara did not even flinch but she was surprised to find there were tears running down her cheeks. 'I've a good mind to throw you off the boat,' she railed at him. 'Send you to her bed, since you like it there so much. Oh, Joe, how could you!'

He got up clumsily, 'Oh, God, I hate this.'

'*You* hate this?' She hiccupped.

'I hate seeing you in tears.' That was the truth. Joe could not bear ever to see her in tears. Then he sat down on the bed again beside her and put his arms round her. For the life of her, Sara could not move away. As if emboldened, he said:

'I know. I know,' soothingly. 'But don't send me away tonight. Please. Besides, it's you I want tonight.'

She caught her breath. 'You have to be joking. If there was anywhere else for you to sleep, believe me you wouldn't be here for another minute.' Yet she must have heard a ring of sincerity in his voice for she shrugged and took off her shoes and tracksuit bottoms and got into bed. 'Just don't touch me,' she said tightly.

Joe put out the light then he got into bed, too. They were both lying on their backs, keeping as far away from each other as possible.

'Do you want to talk any more about it?'

Sara shook her head in the dark.

'Are you asleep?' he asked.

'I just want to forget any of this happened. I want to wake up and find it's all been a dreadful nightmare. But it won't, will it, Joe?'

She heard the rustle as he shook his head in the dark.

'I'm sorry,' he said. It was the first time he had uttered those words.

'Are you?'

'Do you really have to ask that?'

'No. I'm sure you are sorry, now that you've been found out for the liar you are.'

'Sara! No, you're right.'

'Why, Joe? Why did you do it?'

'Do you really have to ask me that? Don't you see, once I had started there was no way I could finish it. There was nothing I could have done that would not have meant I lost you both. Lost everyone, everything. It was like a roller-coaster. You get on one of those and whatever happens you can't get off until it stops.'

'You've never been on a roller-coaster in your life.' Despite herself a small smile crossed Sara's lips.

'I know, because I get sick to my stomach.'

The smile was wiped off as if it had never been. It was a nightmare, but it was not one she would wake from because it was real.

'Go to sleep, Joe. I suppose we'll have to go through this all over again tomorrow and I'm really far too tired to think about it any more just now.'

It seemed to Sara that Joe fell asleep immediately. She drifted in and out of sleep for what was left of the night. There were images of herself with Joe when they were much younger. She woke herself up and suppressed them. There were images of him with Simon. She allowed herself to dwell on those until Joe seemed to fill the frame. She woke herself up and suppressed those. She dreamt of her son — and woke up in a sweat. She tried very hard not to think of what the morning would bring.

Yet habit is a strange thing. As dawn broke, Sara found herself in Joe's arms, lying against him as so often she did, when he was home. Those were times in which she luxuriated as being particularly precious. Had they all been a lie? She stiffened.

'Shh,' murmured Joe. 'Don't go away.'

And Sara stayed.

Chapter Nine

Harriet

There was only a faint glow from Nicola's nightlight in the cabin that the sisters shared. Mindful of her mother's warning, and not wanting to wake Nicola and endure probing questions about the Monopoly game – or anything else for that matter, Harriet picked up Peter Rabbit who had fallen out of bed and tucked him beside the little girl. She stripped off her clothes, deliberately leaving them where they fell, pulled the Pop Idol T-shirt she wore to bed over her head and got under the duvet, where she began to shake, partly from the chill of the bed linen, mostly from shock. Her feet were freezing and she wondered if she would ever be warm again.

She wondered if anything would ever be the same again.

If this summer was a time of delight for Nicola and David – long evenings when it was impossible to get to sleep, bright early mornings when the rest of the world was quiet and the garden was a place of adventure – so far it had been a drag for Harriet.

She had got to know her first boyfriend during the previous year. He had asked her to go to a film with him. They had kissed clumsily a couple of times. It had lasted four weeks. Then, at Christmas, she lost her virginity to a boy from the sixth form with fewer scruples. After all, she had reasoned, it was just too humiliating to be the only virgin left among her friends. The sooner that problem was dealt with the better and Will seemed the best of a not very exciting bunch who was not already one half of an item. Her friends – there were six of them – discussed everything quite openly and all the others had declared that sex was great, fantastic; but though she would never have admitted it, Harriet thought the whole thing was vastly overrated. Very painful the first time and plain messy for the rest, though she rolled her eyes upwards and insisted that it had been – yah – great. (Had the others really told the truth, or were they just saying what they thought everyone wanted to hear? That thought was intriguing, to say the least.)

Will grew tired of her at about the same time that she decided the effort of keeping him a secret from her parents was too great. They parted with relief and hardly any animosity. The hoped-for relationship with her best friend's brother had come to nothing. That was another failure. Unwilling to appreciate that he, at least, was too cautious to become sexually involved with a girl who was not yet sixteen, Harriet eventually found him dull and unresponsive. *Boring*. There had been no one else for some months.

There were the exams, too, but Harriet was sure she had failed those. Her coursework material had come initially from the internet – her father, always generous when it was anything to do with education, had given her a laptop when she started her GCSEs – and though she had changed a few words and phrases here and there once she had retrieved a suitable piece (they all did it, her friends), several efforts had been thrown back at her to do again, the latest with a final warning. Somehow she'd never become very enthusiastic about any of it since. Failed exams would mean retakes unless she could think of a way out, which would be extremely uncool. The one bright spot on her horizon was the holiday. She dreamed it would be crammed with incident. Only half-understanding her own motives, Harriet was actively seeking sexual excitement; up one minute, down the next, she was ripe for any encounter that came her way, the more challenging each time, the more gratifying. The appearance of Simon had been the most exhilarating thing to have happened to her in ages. Not that she would have let him go the whole way. Certainly not the first time. She was quite sure about that. Though she did rather fancy Simon; he'd made her feel special, like she'd got something no other girl had. Even in that short time, she'd known a warm sensation of security with him. In fact, Harriet would have assured any one of her friends prepared to listen that she had actually seen stars when Simon kissed her.

How could she be expected to have to face this? And what, exactly, *was* this?

Between mother and daughter was an unspoken understanding over their treatment of Joe. Harriet had long since ceased to ask why her father chose to stay at home only during the week. To her the weekend was a magical time, like the school holidays when the clock no longer ruled her activities. That he should feel free to indulge in his kind of magic to the exclusion of hers seemed undeserved. Or was it? What had she done, or omitted to do, that had turned her father against her? In her heart, Harriet realized that she was thinking like a drama queen. Her father had given no indication that he felt anything but love and indulgence towards her (except when he criticized her choice of clothes. Didn't all fathers object to what their daughters chose to wear?) Still, he had chosen not to spend his time with her, or with David and Nicola – or with Sara. . . .

She had two friends who lived with one parent and only saw the other, if they did, in the unreal circumstances of a treat – there are only so many times you want to go to the zoo or a museum. There was another who actively hated her step-father. You knew that because her voice went cold and she screwed up her eyes if she had to speak about him. Once Harriet had even dared to mention this but afterwards Kerry hadn't spoken to her for a whole week so she hadn't dared to say anything since. It made you wonder, though.

She knew her father felt in duty bound to Great Aunt Ethel whose black-and-white photograph in a tarnished silver frame stood on her father's desk. Sometimes Harriet actively hated the old lady. The old had a duty to die when they became a burden, she thought passionately and quite ruthlessly.

But if it was true that her father was Simon's father, it must mean that he spent time with him and his mother. The weekends. He had given his magic to them. She turned over, curling herself into a ball, and allowed the tears to seep from her eyes. It was so unfair. Suddenly her sense of family, which on the whole she'd not valued so very much, seemed a fragile thing indeed.

Harriet was woken early by Nicola, who was crooning to Peter Rabbit. Sunlight streamed in through the window. Her first instinct was to leap out of bed and . . . Her second was to burrow under the duvet, her stomach taking a dive through apprehension as she remembered what the day was likely to bring.

'Mum's making bacon'n eggs,' Nicola said, as she heard the rustle above her. 'Get up, lazy-bones.'

'Lazy-bones yourself,' mumbled Harriet, but the smell of bacon was tantalizing and not too unwillingly she allowed herself to be pulled from the top bunk.

'Mum's going to be awful cross when she sees your clothes on the floor.'

'Then you'd better make sure she doesn't.' Harriet stomped off to the bathroom.

Nicola was chattering away happily to her mother, David beside her, when Harriet sidled into her place at the table. There was no sign of their father. Apart from a significant look that Harriet interpreted clearly as *I'll speak to you later*, all Sara said was:

'Sleep well? Eggs with your bacon?'

'I'll just make a bacon sarnie.'

'You do the toast, then.'

'More toast for me,' said David.

'Please,' said Sara out of habit.

'Please.'

'How many pieces?'

'Two. Please,' as an afterthought.

They were still eating when Harriet saw Simon sauntering down the towpath towards them, tall and lithe, young and handsome in the fresh morning light, with a look of – oh yes – a look about him of that youthful Joe in the picture in the polished silver frame on her mother's dressing-table. Involuntarily her eyes met her mother's. She was amazed she had not noticed the resemblance before. Then, why should she, Harriet thought, with a touch of resentment.

Sara got up and went through to the aft deck. After a moment, Harriet followed her.

'Morning, Sara,' Simon called, as if nothing had happened. 'Harriet up yet? Ah. Hi, Harriet.'

Harriet acknowledged the greeting with a casual nod.

'Good morning, Simon,' said Sara, her voice neutral.

Not neutral enough. Simon flushed.

'About last night . . . We . . . There's been a slight communications problem, it seems. That's all it was. Nothing like that'll happen again.'

' 'Course not, Mum,' said Harriet hastily.

'You ready yet?' Simon spoke as naturally as though nothing had happened. 'We'll be leaving in twenty minutes.'

'You're not still going to do all those locks?' Sara exclaimed.

'Might as well. We thought we'd all get out of your way. And Nicola and Davey, too, as we'd planned. They'll be quite safe. Fay said she'd be sure to look after Nicola. And, of course we'd like Mr Moody to come with us.'

'Your mother . . . ?' Sara asked delicately.

'She's going into town to do some shopping. We told her you'd invited her for lunch. She's really looking forward to meeting your Joe,' Simon said, with a relish that bordered on the malicious.

'You haven't . . . ?'

Of course he hadn't, thought Harriet scornfully. She wouldn't mind being a fly on the wall when Amanda arrived for lunch. Though, perhaps not. Much better spend the day at the locks.

'I'm not sure about my father,' Sara said, her voice still flat. 'But I'll make sure everyone else is ready.'

Harriet and Simon worked the locks silently, furiously, only slightly hindered by David, while Henry Moody sat aft with John in the cockpit. But from the young there was none of the shouting or gales of laughter of the previous days. As the *Meadow Skylark* had put-puttered past the *Meadow Sprite* a feeling of relief had flooded Harriet.

'Take over, John, will you?' Simon had said. 'I want to walk.' Without waiting for an answer he leapt for the towpath.

'Me, too,' insisted David, jumping up and down.

'You don't mind, do you?' asked Harriet apologetically, then she and the little boy, more sedately using the gangplank, joined him. Simon soon left them behind, striding the two or three hundred yards that separated each lock of the Bosley Flight with his head down, his hands in his pockets. After a small protest from David they let him go on ahead. Rooks cawed in a small copse but the birds seemed undisturbed by their passing and not one of the humans bothered to observe that, as they climbed steadily into the foothills of the Peak District, the landscape began to fall away below them in a spectacular panorama, shadows and dancing light no less dramatic than their own situation.

A burgeoning tact stayed Harriet's feet some way behind Simon's on the towpath. Her thoughts were chaotic, louring, as dark and tempestuous as the clouds that scudded across the sky to hang over them all. There came a time when David's small hand clutched hers, for the child, too, became sensitive to the atmosphere. Was it tact on Harriet's part, or barely comprehended shyness, the uncertainty of knowing how to behave towards a newly discovered elder brother? Harriet was, suddenly, very unsure of herself. She was so used to being the eldest of the children, the acknowledged heiress of her father's affections. Now she knew where his weekends were spent; that she shared him with a very formidable opponent as her own mother, unknowingly, shared her husband with the woman called Amanda.

So Harriet regarded Simon's back as he walked in front of her, David still silent beside her. She recalled the face of her new-found brother in the moonlight, how she had been filled with a heady excitement that had made her breathless with expectation, an excitement that never would be fulfilled, now. She sighed heavily at the frustration of it all.

'What's the matter?' David asked plaintively. 'Everyone's crotchety this morning.'

'Nothing's the matter, darling,' his sister answered gently. 'Not really. I expect Simon slept badly, that's all.'

'If you ask me, I think Simon got up on the wrong side of the bed,' said David, repeating one of Joe's favourite maxims in a voice even reminiscent of his father's.

Harriet giggled. 'He couldn't have, silly. Bunks only have one side.'

'Well, that's what Dad says,' David insisted stoutly. 'I'm tired,' he announced eventually, his feet lagging.

At the next lock they put him on board and the older two continued on foot, Simon once more out in front, Harriet behind.

The tension between the two eased gradually. There came a moment when Simon stopped.

'I wonder which of our mothers will end up with Joe?' he said.

It had not occurred to Harriet that losing her father altogether was a real possibility. It shocked her immeasurably.

'Whatever.' She shrugged after a minute.

'You don't mean that.'

'Don't I? Like, I mean, who's to say anyone would want him back after what he's done to us.'

'You don't mean that, either.'

'Oh, stop saying what I don't mean,' she snapped.

'Then you'd better admit it's actually all a bit electrifying.'

'That's gross.'

'Like last night?'

Harriet stopped abruptly. 'Was it?' she asked in a small voice. 'Gross, or just bad being found out?'

'Of course, I was a bit shocked,' he said, 'when we were found out. It's not the sort of thing you expect to happen. That is . . .' he hesitated, 'I've hidden from an irate father – once, that is, but I've never been found with a girl by Dad.'

'I'm not allowed out much after nine o'clock,' said Harriet, who suddenly did not want to claim too much sexual experience. 'Dad always insists on coming to fetch me. It's so-o embarrassing.'

'But not as embarrassing as last night.'

'No,' she agreed fervently. There was a pause. 'I suppose you have masses of girlfriends,' she said wistfully.

'A few.' Simon added: 'Not quite as many as I might like. It's the time thing, you know.'

'Exams?'

'And cricket, and my music.'

'You've not mentioned the music before. Cool.'

'I play the drums. Dad bought me a set when I was sixteen. They're really great. I'm with a small group, have been for a couple of years now. We get a few good gigs. What I really need, though, is a van to take the instruments around. I passed my test first time, but I haven't saved enough for one yet. Now this has happened . . .' He left the rest unsaid.

Harriet was thinking that not only did Joe have other people in his life, he had other, expensive, people there, too.

'Still,' said Simon more brightly, 'who knows what might happen now?'

They regarded each other solemnly.

'D'you suppose John knows about Dad?'

'Well, obviously he knows about Dad. He's my uncle.'

'I mean *my* Dad. Um . . . does that make John my uncle, too? Cool.'

'I guess this relationship thing could become difficult.'

After a moment Harriet giggled.

'I don't see much to joke about,' said Simon huffily.

'I just felt like a laugh,' insisted Harriet. 'No law against it, is there?' she ended belligerently. If there was one thing she was not going to stand for, it was an older brother who thought he could boss her around.

Simon snorted. Then he said: 'Someone . . . we should arrange coffee for all of us. I'm perishing.'

'We'll ask Fay at the next lock,' Harriet agreed meekly, choosing not to take offence this time. There was another pause. 'Why're you suddenly in such a bad mood?'

'I'd have thought that after last night any man would be in a black mood.'

105

'Because we . . . because you, like . . . I mean . . .' Harriet stopped, furious with herself. When she was on her own the thoughts and the emotions and the words were so clear in her head. Why was it that whenever she was required to articulate any of them she floundered?

'Whatever.'

'Mum gets furious when I say that,' she said primly.

'So does my mum.'

They both grinned briefly.

Simon sighed. 'At eighteen, a man's supposed to be at the height of his sexual powers, isn't he. Fat chance. I thought this summer was going to be great. And now look what's happened.'

'It's hardly my fault,' said Harriet, aggrieved. Had she really fancied Simon? He didn't seem as kind as she'd first thought and the good looks, boyish charm and openness were probably superficial. 'Don't you have a girlfriend? Amanda – your mum – said something about a girl called Lindy.'

Simon shrugged. 'There's nothing in it, really,' he confessed. 'Um, I'm not really as experienced as I may have sounded.' Harriet took back her supposition that Simon was superficial.

'God, I want to get away. Put all of this . . . mess . . . aside. I don't think I'll ever forgive Dad for this. How dare he take such an unforgivable risk with his children's lives by keeping our existence a secret!'

'Though how could he do otherwise?' asked Harriet shrewdly.

'I wish summer was at an end. I wish . . . But suppose my exam results aren't good enough for me to get away? What then?'

'You don't really expect to fail, do you?'

'I didn't. Now? I'm not sure.'

'Then you'd better be,' said Harriet firmly. 'We've other things to think about just now than your wretched exam results. Just take it that I'm the one who re-sits, you will be going to whichever uni you want.' Simon looked startled, opened his mouth to expostulate, thought better of it and gave his half-sister a placatory grin. 'That's more like it,' said Harriet, sounding so much like an adult that he took her hand and squeezed it.

'You know, having a sister mightn't be such a bad thing, after all.'

'How would you like a ride?' Harriet asked, after a moment's *frisson* of pleasure. 'Um . . . You know, when we were talking about coffee, before? I mean, I suppose someone ought to see if John . . . Sometime this morning. After coffee would be a good time. And someone's got to tell him. I think you should do it.'

'All right,' he agreed, unconsciously squaring his shoulders. 'We'll persuade Nicola to walk with David between the next two locks so I can talk to John.'

The telling was brief. Apparently John seemed neither surprised nor shocked.

'I always knew Joe was up to something,' was his gloomy comment, which Harriet overheard. Her grandfather was there also. Unashamedly she stayed to listen.

'So that's what it's all been about. There it is', said Henry. 'I can't say I won't be glad of the peace and quiet of my sister's house, after this. Best let them sort their own affairs out, in my opinion. I'm far too old for this. It's a sight too complicated for me.'

It was her new aunt, Fay, who surprised Harriet most.

'I've no sympathy for the women,' she said. 'More fool them to have been taken in.'

Harriet thought Fay'd have had more brains to keep that notion to herself.

Chapter Ten

Joe on Joe

I couldn't sleep that night.

Serves you right, are you thinking? I expect it was what I deserved, but that way? Discovering my daughter in the arms of my son? I never did set out to have two secret families. I told you. Whatever I did in the past you can hardly maintain that I deserved that, or for that matter, that those two should have discovered the truth in so stark a fashion.

Of course, in my heart of hearts I knew that my secret life had to be revealed, sometime. Think about it. There are men whose mistresses remain forever hidden or are only exposed to the world for what they are when their lovers die. The old graveyard exposé. Years ago I made ample provision for both of my families, just in case anything happened to me. I never intended that either Amanda or Sara should want for anything. But, hey, I'm still in the prime of life, with years, if not decades, in front of me, I thought it would go on until I was in my grave.

I thought myself one of the fortunate.

After I'd confessed to Sara, I badly wanted solace. And solace, it appeared, was the last thing on Sara's mind.

I broke out into a cold sweat when it came to me in the

middle of the night that they would demand I choose between them, the two bright women I love equally. And I could not tear from my life either the one or the other without destroying myself. Or, most probably, destroying the one who was left. The very tendrils of my heart cling to both, have done so from the start, like a sea creature insidiously winding itself round each one so we are all inextricably entwined. To demand that I root out one would be too high a price to pay. Would be like committing murder.

Yet what alternative is there?

That fine balance I've kept all these years has shifted as I suppose I always knew it must. Suddenly I'm at the top of a dangerous slope, sliding imperceptibly towards a nightmare existence of loneliness, a never-ending icy hell of my own making. Mine is a weak soul, I know that. It requires all the support it can get. Abandoned, forced to abandon one I truly love, I would be doomed.

The first twitters of the dawn chorus, the first glimmer of faint light, eventually told me the night was nearly over, the worst hours past. I had found no solution, come to no decision, but I suppose I've always been an optimist when it comes to relationships. Then, in the way she so often does, Sara rolled over to me sweetly in her sleep. It was the birth of a new day. Cuddling her, I, too, fell into a deep and refreshing sleep.

Waking up was different. I was alone. I could hear Sara in the bathroom. Only a low crooning coming from the girls' cabin indicated that Nicola was awake. I dressed and left the boat. (No, I did not put away the bed and pull out the table. Useless, as usual.) After a while I returned but I couldn't face either the children or the bacon and eggs which I could smell coming from the galley. Once I realised they were going to do as they planned and spend the day on the other boat and everything went quiet, I slunk into the double cabin and collapsed on to the bunk. Cowardly? Of course it was. I merely reasoned that the reckoning would come soon enough. Until then, I'd take whatever repose came my way.

In the event, I dropped into a restless sleep just before midday so that Sara had to rouse me. When she did, she sounded resentful.

'You'd do anything to avoid a row, wouldn't you?'

It is lucky I'm a placid sort of a man and – it must be admitted – like most men I hate rows.

'Joe, I am not going to do your dirty work for you.'

'I don't know what you mean,' I mumbled.

'You'll have to get up, Joe,' she said, loudly and a little impatiently. 'Amanda'll be here soon and you still have to shave. I am not, repeat not, going to be the one to tell her that her husband is also mine.'

She was quite right. I got up reluctantly. I had barely shaved and changed into clean clothes when there was a hail from the bank.

'There she is now. Go on, what are you waiting for!' The push Sara gave me through the door to the aft deck had in it more than a hint of vindictiveness.

Chapter Eleven

Amanda

Years later Amanda was still unable to decide when it was that she knew the truth about Joe. That morning she had decided to remain behind when Fay and her brother took the young people through the locks on the *Meadow Skylark*. There was shopping to do, she told them. She thought she'd wander round for a bit before lunch.

'Since when did you go in for shopping, Mum?' asked Simon.

'Since I have an hour or so for myself,' she retorted, thinking how long since that had been. 'Afterwards there's a book I've been trying to finish. I can always find somewhere to sit in the sun until lunch.'

'If your mother wants a quiet day, don't argue,' insisted John.

'I'm sure if Amanda doesn't want to come, she needn't,' added Fay, and Amanda almost changed her mind.

'Besides, Sara does seem very keen that you should have lunch with them,' added Simon. 'It would be rude to disappoint her.'

She had looked at him wondering why the comment seemed

loaded but he had returned her gaze unblinkingly so she thought she must be mistaken. Once they had all gone, Amanda walked along the towpath until she found a shop which sold fresh bread and bottles of milk. She put the groceries into a coolbag and had a cursory glance at the other shops nearby but, after all, there was nothing there that inspired her to linger so she returned to the towpath where she found a conveniently sited bench-seat in the sun. Here she sat and read until it was time for her to make her way to the *Meadow Sprite.*

It was a pity she was not able to make herself more presentable before she turned up for lunch, she was thinking as she reached the narrow-boat. Still, Sara would understand why, and hopefully Sara's Joe wouldn't notice that she felt hot and sweaty from all that time in the sun. She was actually poised with her foot on the gangplank when she was confronted by a familiar figure. Joe. Her Joe. He was not a figment of her imagination, looming above her from the cock- pit of the *Meadow Sprite.* There was absolutely no doubt about it, this was her husband, on another narrow-boat (when she thought he was at a conference), and with another woman standing beside him.

No one said a word. Then Sara picked up a bottle of gin from a tray balanced on the roof of the narrow-boat.

'I think you'd better come aboard and have a drink.'

Amanda, her limbs disjointed from the shock of the encounter, wobbled across the gangplank.

'Woops,' said Joe, grabbing her by the arm. 'Careful, we don't . . .'

Amanda glared at him, thought about basilisks.

Sara looked as though she knew precisely what Amanda was thinking.

'Give me the shopping,' she said. 'Sorry about this.' She poured a generous slug of gin into a glass. 'You'd better sit down. Tonic?' When Amanda nodded silently, she dribbled a centimetre of tonic on to the gin. 'There's lemon, but we're out of ice, I'm afraid. The children took all of it.'

'You've only poured two,' said Joe. 'Dear,' he added as an afterthought.

Sara froze him with a glare. 'You don't drink gin.' Then she shrugged and walked through to the galley, emerging with a coolbag. She handed Joe a bottle of lager.

Amanda who so far had not spoken a word, thought she was taking the situation very well. Or just maybe it was the gin that was anaesthetizing her. She found it quite impossible to look directly at Joe, who also did not appear to have anything to say for himself.

'I suppose you've known about this – me – all along,' Amanda said eventually to Sara. Her voice was husky and she gasped as though she was short of breath. It was outrageous, an appalling thought that Sara had known about her existence all this time – however long this time had been.

'Of course not,' said Sara indignantly. 'Do you think I could have spent time with you, enjoyed time with you, if I had known about you? Whatever you might think about me, I'm not devious.'

She was convincing, Amanda conceded. 'You don't really mean you only found out about Joe last night?' she said, at the end of a long drawn-out sigh. 'Like me?' Joe, with another woman. With another *family*. 'How did you find out?' she asked faintly.

'Joe and I found Simon with Harriet. She was late back.'

Amanda registered the incredulity on Sara's face even though her words were matter-of-fact.

'You found the two together? So, what were they doing, going for a walk?'

'Not exactly.'

'How, not exactly?'

113

'Best left alone, dear.'

Both women glared at Joe.

Amanda decided not to pursue that topic of conversation.

It was the mention of the circumstances that had brought all this to a head that brought Joe back to life.

'What in God's name possessed you to come on a canal holiday, anyway?' he growled at Amanda. 'Especially when I was away,' he added, as if attack were the best part of a poor defence.

'Joe, how dare you try to put me in the wrong. Yes, you were away. Simon and I decided we wanted a holiday. We decided we wanted to come here. You had already decided it was not the sort of holiday you would contemplate – or so you led us to believe. It was my money we used, mine and Simon's, and John's and Fay's. Not yours. How . . . how was I to know you'd . . . you'd be here with your mistress?' She spat at him, though her eyes remained at the level of his top button. 'You told me you were going to London for the conference.'

'Joe goes to a business conference in late August,' said Sara.

'Ah. Of course,' said Amanda. 'Not a conference, though. Our holiday.'

Joe returned to the attack. 'How many other times have you gone away when I thought you were all safe at home?' he demanded. 'And where has all this money come from, I'd like to know?'

Amanda shrugged. 'I have a job.'

'Oh, come on,' he said. 'Since when?'

'Since a few years ago, actually,' she answered, her voice shrill, stung by his derisive tone. 'I just never bothered to tell you about it. Like you never bothered to tell me about . . . about . . .' She stopped. Took a deep breath. No. She was damned if she was going to cry.

'Well, I know you give the primary school a few hours occasionally. It's not a proper job, though, is it?'

Amanda gritted her teeth. Now was not the moment to explain to Joe the nature of her employment but she was not going to be wrong-footed, either.

'As a matter of fact, this is the first time we've ever gone away without you. But you . . .' she began to feel angry. Healthily angry. 'You even sound self-righteous about blaming me. As though what you've done doesn't come into the category of unfaithfulness at all.'

'You're so right. It doesn't,' he answered flatly.

Sara leant forward to splash more gin into Amanda's glass. Then she added tonic to her own glass. Amanda was aware that Sara's hand was unsteady for all she was drinking less. Her own knuckles were clenched into fists on the table, as though she really was spoiling for a fight. Sara placed her hand over one of the fists, as if to offer meagre comfort, if not moral support. Amanda tensed at the touch, then she relaxed, throwing Sara an enigmatic glance, recognizing that they ought to be allies. Then she drained her glass. Sara got up.

'Coffee anyone?' There was no reply. 'Maybe cold sobriety is not the way to get over the next few hours.' She fetched bread, cheese and pickles and placed them on the table with plates and knives and a bowl of apples while the other two remained sitting at the table, studiously avoiding each other's eyes. She emptied the bottle of gin into Amanda's glass and threw it into the bin. Then she opened another can of beer for Joe.

Joe cut a thick slice of bread for himself, took a hunk of cheese and a couple of pickled onions. Amanda picked at the small slice of bread which Sara had cut for her, crumbling it on her plate, watching the man eat. When he had speared the last of his onion and pushed the plate away, she said quietly:

'I guess I've always known there was something. Probably someone else.'

'You what?' Joe expostulated.

'Oh, come on,' Amanda snapped. 'Do you take me for a

115

complete fool? How many couples do you know who lead the sort of life we've done for the past umpteen years? It was obvious.' No, there had been none of the classic signs, as she remembered once explaining to her brother. There were no lipstick marks, no strange handkerchiefs. There was no atmosphere between them, not even a diminution of their sexual life. Of course there had been something. It was the very fact that his life was so ordered, that whatever happened he kept rigidly to his own agenda.

'No, it wasn't,' Joe said stubbornly. 'Or you'd have challenged me.'

'Why should I? You always came back to me at the weekend. You were always very attentive to me, at the weekend . . .'

'Probably in the same way he was to me, during the week,' Sara broke in.

A hint of red stained the cheekbones of the man who sat between them, otherwise poker-faced.

'How did you manage it, Joe?' asked Sara. 'I never found anything incriminating in all those years.'

'Two identical sets of everything,' he answered promptly, almost proudly. 'You were never meant to find out.'

'So what was the use of complaining?' Amanda continued. 'Besides . . .' then she stopped.

'Besides what?' Joe wanted to know.

Amanda examined the nail of her left thumb minutely.

'Besides . . . Here's a revelation for you,' she said, her tone loaded with self-mockery. 'I was always so afraid that you'd never come back if I complained.' Then she put her head on her arms and began to cry softly.

She was aware of Joe moving uneasily beside her. He patted her shoulder clumsily. She knew he hated tears, and that he could not imagine what she was talking about.

'I can't imagine why you should think that. We may not

have gone through a legal ceremony, but we're as good as married. I regard us as being married,' he said robustly.

'In the same way that we are?' asked Sara quietly.

'Exactly. No piece of paper, but a commitment.'

'I don't see how a man can commit to two women at once,' said Sara.

Though in an odd way Amanda could understand it.

'Joe wouldn't marry me because he said he wasn't the marrying kind.'

'Why do women allow themselves to be taken in by that statement?'

'I think that was my reaction. It was certainly that of my parents. But I got pregnant. In those days things were different for girls who got pregnant,' Amanda said kindly to Sara, as if the gap between their ages was considerably more than it was. 'Well, they still were for my family. The divorce was bad enough for them. Putting them through an illegitimate grandchild would have been traumatic. It was just as well we moved to South Wales. And I admit I was weak enough to call myself Mrs Williams rather than suffer the social stigma of being unmarried.'

'We never went through a marriage ceremony,' Sara observed quietly. 'I always knew Joe would never marry me because he told me so. We staged it for my parents.'

'You see, because you were only ever home at the weekend, I was afraid you'd leave us altogether if you were not content with us. You had so many opportunities for comparisons.'

'You don't seem to have a very high opinion of the man you live with, either of you,' Joe said.

That wasn't true. Amanda opened her mouth, then she closed it. His voice had sounded aggrieved, to her surprise, but now was not the time to tell him that she had always thought very highly of him.

'I can't imagine why you're surprised,' she said flatly.

117

'All right,' he said. 'So I know I'm married to neither of you. What do we do now? Even if I were to go against principles of a lifetime, I couldn't marry you both.'

'Principles!'

'On the other hand, you still have certain responsibilities towards the children,' Amanda pointed out. 'After all these years.'

'You know I would never deny it, or them.'

'I was thinking more of Sara's children,' said Amanda. 'They're so much younger than Simon, who is about to leave home anyway.'

'And I'm pregnant again.' Sara said it so matter-of-factly that at first Amanda thought she'd not heard it correctly. 'It's an afternoon of revelations, isn't it?' Sara shrugged. 'You might as well hear it all. I'm pregnant again. No alcohol,' she raised her glass, 'can't stand it again. It was always the first sign, wasn't it. Before the days of test kits.'

'When?' demanded Joe, leaning forward.

He was pleased. Genuinely pleased, Amanda noticed with interest. She remembered that he'd enjoyed her pregnancy far more than she ever had. It was just the tiny baby he couldn't cope with. Been frightened of, in a way.

'Three months,' Sara said. 'So I shall need your support. For a time. Just until the baby's old enough for me to go out and get a job.'

'Now, there's no need for that kind of talk,' Joe objected hurriedly.

'And that is no reason for abandoning Amanda.'

'Abandoning Amanda? Who's talking about abandoning anyone,' Joe said indignantly. 'Of course I have every intention of continuing to support you both.'

'Well, thanks.' Amanda smiled sweetly.

'I'm going to make some tea,' said Sara.

'Let me . . .' Both Joe and Amanda spoke together.

Sara laughed. 'I could get used to that,' she said, though not unkindly. 'But I think you may safely save that sort of thing for a little longer.'

Nevertheless, Joe followed Sara into the galley. Amanda made no move to join them. For one thing, it was their boat, she was in the position of guest. For another she did not think she had the ability to move.

When Sara returned with three mugs of tea, Amanda realized what it was about Joe's mistress – his other mistress, the thought came into her mind with shocking clarity – that had been puzzling her ever since she first saw Sara at the top of the gangplank that morning. She might be looking at a younger version of herself. Their colouring was almost identical: hair and eyes, cheekbones and shape of chin proclaimed them almost-sisters. Had Joe, all those years ago, been consciously looking for a less tired version of his wife? Or had the advent of Sara totally bowled him over because she reminded him so much of the woman he was living with? And which of the two options would she rather had happened? For the life of her, Amanda could not say.

'Why is it I get the feeling you are both glad of an excuse to get rid of me?' Joe said mournfully.

The two women looked at each other involuntarily and laughed with genuine amusement.

'Oh, I wouldn't say that, exactly,' Sara replied.

'Only, you could hardly expect us to go on just as before, could you?' Amanda said reasonably. 'Not now that we know the truth.'

'It seems to me that you, for one, have concealed a lot. Whatever did you want to go and get a job for? I don't keep you short. You've always had whatever you've wanted, clothes, things for the house.'

'Boredom.' She shrugged. 'A need to assert myself. A desire to spend what was mine.'

119

'But why the deception? Why did you never tell me you wanted a job?'

'Why did you never tell me you wanted another woman?'

'Don't . . .' Sara began, and stopped.

'What sort of a job is it, anyway?' Joe demanded, as if Sara had not interrupted.

'As you know, I'm not exactly over-qualified,' Amanda replied wryly. 'But I found that I am still needed at the school. I do a lot more than an hour or so. I'm a full-time primary assistant. What is more, I'm seriously considering doing a teaching qualification.'

'That degree?' asked Sara.

'Probably,' answered Amanda, for whom the decision was becoming more of a certainty by the minute.

'As if,' Joe said derisively.

There was an appalled silence.

Sara looked from one to the other, her mouth slightly open. Amanda knew that there was a crackle of electricity between herself and Joe which was almost palpable. His eyes glittered dangerously, and she was aware that her cheeks were flushed, and not from the gin. If ever Sara had the slightest notion that their relationship was not a fully sexual one, Amanda knew she was dismissing it then.

The tension eased.

'Anyway, it's plain we can't go on as we are,' Sara said, into the silence. 'For one thing, it wouldn't be fair on the children.'

The children.

'I suppose they'll be back soon,' Amanda commented, consulting her watch. 'I think, if you don't mind, I'd like to lie down for a bit before I have to face them.'

'Use one of the end bunks,' Sara suggested. 'It's quieter down there. And I'll keep them out of your way for as long as I can.'

The *Meadow Skylark* returned and moored just below them. The little children ran across the *Meadow Sprite*'s gangplank, clamouring for their tea. Amanda could hear Sara shushing them and saying that she would feed them on baked beans and toast. Soon after, she made her escape without having to say more than good night to Joe.

Back in the *Meadow Skylark* Amanda nursed an aching head. Nauseated by food, she drank several cups of black coffee and retired to bed – where she was to suffer for it, tossing and turning through the night, the caffeine and her storm-tossed emotions causing her heart to thump almost unbearably and a fine sweat to break out on her neck and between her breasts.

John came to the rescue, reasoning shrewdly that Harriet was the one most likely to be hurt by the tense atmosphere. Though nothing had been said about just how intimately Joe's older children were involved in what was a bizarre situation – Joe's knowing both women – he thought he guessed a part of it. So after supper he suggested another game of Monopoly and sent Fay to fetch Harriet from the *Meadow Sprite*. Released, Harriet came willingly and the riotous game that followed broke any ice that remained between the youngsters, establishing in its place a natural camaraderie. It is not easy to stay on your high horse when you have bought and sold hotels, collected rent on Park Lane and bartered your railway stations for Piccadilly.

The lull of time suspended could not last. Some sort of a resolution had to be found, and before they parted. After lunch the next day, Joe announced that they would be mooring early on their southward journey. They moored before they reached the centre of Stoke-on-Trent. It was quiet and it was also warm, with the sun playing on the ripples where a fish had risen, warming the backs of a family of ducks, the brood of young bobbing on the surface like fluffy corks.

When both boats were secure, Joe handed John two bank-notes.

'Think you can occupy everyone until bedtime?' he asked, and when they had gone, all except Henry, who retired with a paperback to the privacy of the cockpit aft in the other boat, he put the kettle on.

'Clear heads we need, this time,' he said directly.

'You think we might have something to celebrate, eventually?'

They took mugs of tea, biscuits and cushions to the forward deck and settled down. 'What do you want to do when we get home?' Joe asked.

Neither of the women answered, Amanda because she wanted to keep all her options open. She was not sure about Sara. In the dark watches of the night her mind had looped round Joe and Simon and what was going to happen to herself. An idea had come to her eventually, but she had dismissed it almost as it formed. It was impossible, ridiculous, out of the question.

'If you like,' Joe suggested cautiously, 'we could continue as though nothing had happened. I mean, share out the week as before. Perhaps that would be the best thing—'

'Certainly not,' both women declared simultaneously, though both were looking at Joe and not each other.

'You can't mean . . . you don't mean you are both thinking of throwing me out? I mean . . . where would I go?'

Amanda sighed. 'It's what you deserve, but I suppose not,' she replied.

'No,' agreed Sara, eventually. 'But isn't that just like a man,' she exclaimed wrathfully, 'He's unfaithful, unrepentant, and still expects us to fall over backwards to accommodate him.'

Joe glowered.

Amanda said hastily: 'But for the sake of the children . . .'

Sara snorted. Then she sighed, too.

'Oh, all right. For the children's sake.'

'Good. We continue as we are, for the children's sake,' repeated the much-relieved Joe.

'But only while we decide what to do in the long term,' said Amanda firmly.

'Just for the time being,' reiterated Sara.

'Do you really want to change things?' Joe challenged Amanda.

'Of course things have to change. I told you. There's my job. Simon will be off our hands soon, and then what will I do?'

'I'd really love the chance to have a large garden,' said Sara wistfully, unexpectedly, showing that she, too, had been wakeful in the middle of the night. 'But how can I, with the children, not to mention the new baby?'

'It seems to me that what we both want is a chance of leading the other's life,' said Amanda, slowly.

'You mean, just swap?' said Joe, incredulously.

'Irresistible . . . impracticable . . . preposterous,' said Sara, regretfully.

'I didn't mean it quite like that. But an idea did come to me in the early hours. Not a particularly original one, not in some parts of the world, I mean. You see, what we need is not two households, but one.' Silence followed Amanda's statement.

'That's absurd,' scoffed Joe, unconvincingly.

'Intriguing, but not very sensible,' Sara objected.

Of course Amanda had not thought it out, not in any detail. It had just seemed something worth exploring as dawn broke and her mind had stilled just before sleep. In the cold light of day – even sitting in the sun – she could see the snags only too clearly. It was unthinkable. Or was it?

'First of all there are the children,' she said resolutely. 'Then there's the sex.'

'Amanda,' protested Joe, pink to the ears.

'So?' she asked calmly. 'You're not suggesting that you haven't wanted to make love to each of us since yesterday morning, are you?'

His lips twitched. 'No,' he said. 'And very nice it would have been too.'

The declaration seemed to clear the air.

'Right, then. Now in other parts of the world, the senior wife takes it upon herself to find a suitable junior wife for her husband. One he will love but, most importantly, one who will fit into her household.'

'You're proposing . . . no, really,' Joe spluttered. 'You mean to tell me you don't . . . any more?'

'Don't be a fool, dear,' said his first wife sweetly. 'Besides, we're not in those parts of the world and you've already made Sara your choice. I'm just thinking that we should – regularize the situation.'

'You mean, as in inviting me to live with you?' asked Sara suspiciously. 'As a *junior* wife?'

'Hardly,' Amanda replied quickly. 'But to set up a household together. With equal rights.'

'Regarding Joe, too?'

'Think of us as the two couples we were,' Amanda continued persuasively. 'Would either of us have wanted to throw Joe out forty-eight hours ago? We have a good thing. Why spoil it for the sake of convention?'

'We *had* a good thing,' said Sara darkly.

'And it's gone for ever?' demanded Joe, his aplomb recovered. 'Honestly? You can truthfully say that?' Amanda looked across at Sara and surprised a blush starting on the other woman's neck. So her idea was not so extraordinary, after all. What a nerve the man had, to have gone so casually from one to the other all these years. She supposed he had made Sara feel just as much missed, desired, as he had made her, each weekend. And why should she forgo that?

'There's the baby, too. But to share, openly?' Sara giggled nervously.

'You have a point,' she admitted ruefully. 'And it does have its funny side.'

'So by not splitting up,' Joe said, 'there is a chance you could both end up happier?'

'Ye-es.' They said it cautiously.

'Still without any ceremony,' Joe said, 'again. We'd have to move, of course. Then the neighbours needn't know. About us. We could be relatives . . .'

'Once you start inventing, all kinds of complications arise, Joe,' Amanda reminded him gently.

'There's . . .' he stopped.

The women both looked at him enquiringly.

'We could have a large house with a big garden, I suppose,' he said, after a pause.

'Grow our own vegetables.' Sara began elaborating. 'We could even keep chickens. I've always wanted to keep chickens.'

'Have you? I never knew that.'

'And I could do a full-time degree,' said Amanda. 'Then get a proper teaching job. A meal to come home to. Bliss. Sorry, Joe. It hasn't all been bad.'

For another moment it looked as though Joe was about to say something else. Then he said:

'There's just one problem. What do we tell the children?'

Chapter Twelve

Joe on Joe

Do you ever think that we carry the seeds of our own destruction within us?

I think we must. Like that morning when I left the canal holiday brochure under my bedside table by accident.

There was a moment that afternoon when another narrowboat glided past us. Its windows were open to catch the breeze and a woman was relaxing in the saloon listening to music. As the sonorous chords drifted across, I recognized the Rachmaninov second concerto.

Sara and Amanda also recognized it in the same moment. It was not surprising, for that piece has been a favourite of ours for ever. They exchanged a glance and I knew what was coming.

'There was a weekend in the spring when I heard that piece,' said Amanda.

I laughed uneasily. 'Classic FM's always playing it, along with the Grieg.' They also knew which one of Grieg's works I meant.

'It was at the time when I discovered I was pregnant again,' said Sara, nodding as though she, too, knew exactly what Amanda was getting at.

'When we first thought of a canal holiday. I remember you were dead against it, Joe.'

I shrugged uncomfortably. 'Guess I changed my mind.'

'There was a dedication that intrigued me so much I couldn't forget it,' Amanda persisted relentlessly.

'*And for my other family . . .*' said Sara quietly. 'It followed the Grieg.'

'That's the one.'

There was a pause. Then Amanda continued:

'Was it you, Joe? Did you send in that dedication?'

'And if so, which of us was the *other* family?'

1 opened my mouth and nothing emerged.

'If the DJ had said: *"For my two families"*, I'd have thought nothing of it.'

'Nor I.'

'I can't answer that,' I told them. And that was the truth. 'It just happened that way.'

Was it a death wish? Did I already know that the deception had run its course? Was I just plain tired of it all? Was that why I gave in to an impulse?

'Well, that's been bugging me ever since,' said Sara.

'I'm glad we've sorted that out.'

I really don't know what I expected from that confrontation, the attack, the recriminations. Yes, I do. I thought they'd tip me into the canal. Joking apart, maybe that's what I secretly hoped would happen. So that I could run away. That would have been so easy. The in-depth analysis thing was what scared me.

It hurt that neither of them seemed to have a very high opinion of me, despite their insisting otherwise. I could see it in their faces, disillusionment being the worst. Yet after all those years we'd been together, it seemed to me we were a lot happier than many other couples we knew. Though when I say that, I have to admit we – that is, both Amanda and I, and

Sara and I – have few close friends. I certainly have no male friend with whom I share more than the most banal of confidences over a pint. (Is that a form of self-protection?) Anyway, you know what I mean. We were solid. How could we live apart after all the good times?

How could I be cast aside like an old sock? Is that what my hurt was all about? Pride?

I wanted to tell them that I couldn't marry them both, even though that was what I'd have liked, even given my previous aversion to formal marriage. Fortunately the words stuck in my throat. I'd only been joking about running away. The very thought that I might abandon them, or any of the children, was totally abhorrent.

There was the new baby. Now that was a thing. A new baby.

I know what you're thinking. I didn't do well by Amanda and Simon, so why should I be expected to do any better with a new baby? No reason at all, except that I am older. Grant me that I have learnt something from life. And I do love the children, did love them, even when they were babies and the responsibility of them terrified me.

Amanda. I said that I thought she'd been diminished by being left, that time. I only ever thought it of her once. Make no mistake, she's robust. At least, that's what I've always thought. It came as a real surprise to find out that she's always been afraid I'd leave again. I couldn't have done that to her, just left without a word, even if there had ever come a time when I wanted out – which I never have. And now I find out she's been working at that school for years. She's been earning money there.

All right. I admit I'm one of the world's chauvinists when it comes to women working when they have a child to bring up.

It must have been almost as hard for her to hide it from me as it was for me, remembering to keep alive my saga about Aunt Ethel.

You remember Aunt Ethel, of course?

So why, when it was an afternoon of revelation, did I not mention my other secret, that Aunt Ethel had died some years before? I don't know.

Yes, I do. I need Aunt Ethel. That's to say, just at the moment I don't have any real need for her, but something tells me that in the future she might be very useful.

What next? You may well ask. Amanda was right. If I'd had the slightest encouragement, I would have made love to both of them. (Not both at once. Though . . . no, of course not.) They are both very beautiful women – each in her own way – and I can't imagine life without either of them. And that is the truth.

John's a good chap. We've had our differences, but you can always rely on him when there's a spot of bother. He took the children off without a murmur – though I think Fay would have given her eye-teeth to have had an excuse to stay. Neither of them said a word out of place but you could see they were aching to know what was going on.

Had I really thought Amanda and Sara would consider carrying on as before? In the middle of the night it had seemed a good idea. In the morning I could see it wouldn't work. When I was with Amanda, Sara's shadow would be there and when I was with Sara, the shadow of Amanda would come between us. In the end we would be forced apart out of suspicion and bitterness.

How about the bombshell that Amanda had dropped? That we should join our households, become one family? It's crazy. How could it possibly work! *Two women* in the same house? Sharing me? I'd be like the bone between two dogs. All the same you have to admire the audacity of it.

We would have to move. Buy a bigger house. In the present state of the housing market that would be no bad thing.

If we go ahead with this scheme, I still think my point

about keeping it from the neighbours would be a good idea – though I suppressed a twinge of conscience with difficulty when Amanda began talking about inventions – Aunt Ethel, that vital component of my secret life.

What we told the children was an expurgated version of the truth. It appeared we needn't have worried, for friends and school were the main concerns, for David and even Nicola soon settled. Simon merely grunted. Already he seems to have grown away from us. Let's pray his results are what he wants. His main, declared, concern was for transport. 'I'll really need wheels, now.'

By mutual, tacit consent, the families separated. I was now fully recovered and able to work the locks, though Simon and John, leading us through, made sure the gates were left ready for us to enter.

The last day of the *Meadow Sprite*'s trip started miserably cold and wet, but as an augury of things to come a pale, watery sun emerged from the greyish clouds just as we approached Great Hayward. I continued for a mile or so to where there was a turning circle at Tixall Wide. There we moored for the night.

I was restless. I dragged everyone off the boat for a walk. Another narrow-boat was moored nearby, old, unconverted, with a top plank running the length of the hold over which canvasses were strapped. On the roof of the tiny cabin was displayed canal furniture: jugs, buckets, drinking-mugs for sale, all painted with vivid roses and castles on black or green backgrounds. There was also a large brown Mesham pottery teapot, its lid a small replica of itself, and beside that polished brasses tied in strings.

'Pretty,' exclaimed Nicola, enchanted.

'Why castles?' wondered Sara aloud.

I'd read up on it. 'Lost in the mists of time,' I explained.

'They're either a Romany tradition or they're meant to represent the kilns of the potteries through which the canals run, or they might even be just the dream houses of the canal men's families, which would tie in with the roses theme, of course.'

'I like the roses best,' said Nicola.

It seemed to presage the new life to come. On impulse I said:

'We'll buy something, and give it pride of place in the new home.'

Chapter Thirteen

Sara

When she arrived home after the canal holiday, Sara developed bad morning sickness which, for a few days, carried on into the evening — she'd never been one for doing things the usual way. To her credit, Harriet took charge, insisting that her mother should go to bed, which Sara did thankfully. Then Harriet pleaded with the local surgery for a visit from the district midwife, who came, wheedled from her patient that she had recently learnt that her husband had been having an affair, prescribed something mild (which Sara promptly threw away), and promised to visit in a week or so. Which promise was not kept, but Sara was back on her feet by then, so it didn't matter.

Lying motionless in bed, trying to persuade her baby not to upset her equilibrium, Sara wondered how had she missed the signs? How could she have been so naïve as to believe that Joe spent the whole weekend with Aunt Ethel? For now that she knew the truth, it was obvious that all he had to do was spend an hour or so with the old lady, then the rest of the weekend he could devote to Amanda and Simon.

It was atrocious that he had kept hidden the existence of his firstborn, whatever you might feel about Amanda.

132

Amanda. She had warmed to Amanda instinctively.

Then, there was that appalling episode with Simon and Harriet. What might have happened if she and Joe had not arrived when they did? Sara's blood ran cold while the bile rose in her throat and she had to dash to the bathroom, yet again. By the time she had finished retching she had decided not to go down that path (whatever she meant by that). Harriet had assured her that nothing in particular had happened and Sara chose to believe her daughter, for the sight of a parent so aghast by the fraternization of his two children whom he had hitherto managed to keep hidden from each other was traumatic enough. So, in her debilitated state, she rationalized.

The midwife had asked her if she intended leaving her husband. A not so inconsiderable part of Sara thought that was no bad idea. *But I am a coward*, she admitted miserably. There were the three other children who needed looking after, let alone the coming baby, even if Joe kept his word that he would continue to support them all.

There was Joe himself. For all his faults, misdemeanours, transgressions – call them what you would – she still loved him. He had been willing to accommodate her into his life. It had been on her suggestion that they had begun living together all those years ago. She had wanted him so badly it had hurt. She could not begin to imagine life without him. Joe could simply have gone into an affair, then left her, with or without a child. As for now, secretaries were two a penny. The office work she did for Joe was neither here nor there. That he had chosen to stay with her and bring up three children had to count for something. Surely?

But setting up house with Amanda, sharing Joe . . . That was outrageous.

This is my home, Sara thought, a week or so later, staring out of the kitchen window at the small patch of back garden she had spent hours cultivating. There were a few roses and shrubs but a good-sized patch of vegetables and salad crops which provided the family with almost all its needs – she bought soft fruit as she had not been able to persuade Joe to put in a proper fruit cage. She sniffed the fragrance of baking that was coming from her gas-cooker. Setting up house with Amanda couldn't possibly work. She and Amanda would be at each other's throats as soon as they were forced to share a kitchen. Miserably, Sara heaved, and fled yet again to the bathroom.

In the end, Sara decided that the benefits of being looked after during her pregnancy outweighed the immensity of changing her life so radically. If they could all live together amicably it might even be worthwhile. If not, there was nothing to stop her from leaving when she was good and ready.

Did Amanda feel the same? It was something Sara could not quite bring herself to ask on the infrequent occasions when they spoke after that holiday. It had been Amanda's idea; Joe had agreed with alacrity, so she would just go along with it.

It was Sara who galvanized Amanda into making the first, most radical change by challenging her on her determination to become a teacher.

'Were you serious, or was it a Joe thing?' she demanded, one afternoon in October when Amanda came to visit her – bringing with her new-born-baby clothes in a tactful yellow.

'I don't know what you mean,' Amanda temporized.

'Yes, you do. As in Joe defiance? Yesterday I logged on to a website which gave all sorts of information about how you might get started. Here, I wrote it down for you.' She passed Amanda a small piece of paper on which she had written down the information. Amanda did not seem interested, Sara thought, but she folded the paper and put it into her bag carefully enough all the same. 'Only the thing is, you may have to decide fairly quickly your way to go if you want to start a course next year.'

'I'm not sure that I do.'

'Why? What's happened to make you change your mind?'

'I don't think I'll ever become qualified.'

'Not without some work, that's true, but what does that matter if it's what you would like to do for the rest of your working life. And think of the pension,' she ended. 'Besides, you'd be good at it.'

'What makes you say that?'

'It's obvious you get on with children. You've been working with them for years, which has to look good on a CV. You're enthusiastic. I know that from what you've told me about the things you do in school. You're well organized and patient. . . .'

'Not so sure about that,'

'Of course you are, and you have a great sense of humour.'

'That's certainly been in abeyance recently.'

'I thought you'd risen above that.'

'Above Joe?' Amanda raised her eyebrows.

'If it does it for you.' Sara grimaced as the baby kicked her and did a somersault.

'Footballer?'

'Probably a gymnast. So, are you going to think about it?'

Amanda had thought about it, and discussed it with her head teacher, as she later told Sara.

'For the moment I'll still be working at my school but I've been accepted to do a one-year-access course in Newport to do A-levels in maths, English and French, starting next September and I've got until the December to apply for an ITT place in Caerleon the following academic year. That's Initial Teacher Training, to you.'

'My,' said Sara, admiringly. 'That sounds like an awful amount of work in one year.' Not the way she'd want to go.

'But at least I've got until then to bring my very rusty French up to standard. And I might try to find a tutor for the maths. I think I might even specialize in maths teaching when I'm qualified. It would help to find a job, maths being such an unpopular core subject. But that decision I can really leave for some months.'

It took Joe four months to find a house which, on paper, exactly fitted their requirements: large enough to accommodate the two families and with a bit of land. Ty Mawr was an old Welsh longhouse, a stone farmhouse set in three acres, part of which was orchard, in a village not far from Monmouth. It was badly in need of decoration, the kitchen was so old it was practically retro, though it was equipped with a gas-fired Aga which heated the water; the only bathroom needed updating – they had plans for two more, eventually – and there was no proper central heating. But the roof was new, the timbers were sound and along with apple and pear trees there was already a well-stocked kitchen garden.

Each woman thought of the unfamiliar with trepidation. Sara, in an advanced stage of what had become a troublesome pregnancy full of discomfort, swelling ankles, excess weight gain and raised blood pressure, viewed the impending move with horror.

'Dareth and I will do all the heavy stuff.' Joe had found an unemployed local lad who was happy to be taken on as casual labour for the time being, decorating both inside and out being a priority. Amanda would be in charge of the kitchen, with Harriet's help, until Sara was ready to take over. 'We'll master the Aga if it kills us!' During the school holidays this would be no problem. Joe had promised them a cleaning lady once term started. 'So all Sara has to do is put her feet up until the baby is born.'

'Do you realize how soon that is?' exclaimed Sara. 'And what happens afterwards? Tiny babies can't cope with dust and commotion.'

'Don't worry.' With what was an infuriatingly complete trust in his own judgement, Joe refused to see obstacles where he maintained there was none. 'It feels right in my bones.'

'What does Amanda say?'

'She agrees with me.'

Too exhausted to delve further, Sara permitted herself to be convinced.

'It will be a seven-day wonder when we all move, there's no getting away from it, but it'll pass. We'll have the villagers eating out of our hands in no time.'

Sara was dubious. Amanda was far too busy with her job and her course work. If anyone had the locals eating out of her hands, she thought, it would have to be her. There was another matter troubling her.

'I wish I could believe Nicola and David will settle at the new school. You know what children are like. I should hate to think they'd be bullied because of us.'

'Sara, they are not going to be punished for the sins of their parents,' Joe said firmly. 'As for Harriet, she can look after herself.'

There was something – someone else bothering her. 'What have you told Aunt Ethel? Joe, you have told her, about us?'

'Aunt Ethel's known about us all since the beginning,' he said gently.

'Goodness. Has she really? What does she think?'

'In the beginning she was furious. I talked her round.'

'You didn't.'

'Actually, I told her that if she wanted me to continue looking after the factory she had to accept me as I am.' He shrugged. 'She chose to make the best of it.'

'Is that why we've never met her?'

'She's a very proper lady. Accepting a situation is one thing, being social about it is another.'

'So we still won't get to see her?'

'I doubt it.' He hesitated. 'Besides, she's not been at all well recently. I thought Fridays might be a good day to go and visit her. If that's all right with you and Amanda?'

'Of course,' she said woodenly. It would have to be.

In mid-December four adults, two teenagers and two smaller children descended on Ty Mawr. They moved in in the wet and the rain never stopped until Boxing Day. As Sara had expected, the whole exercise was complete hell. But after the first twenty-four hours it was apparent that the roof didn't leak, the new window-frames could withstand the rivulets that streamed down the glass and splashed on to the solid new sills. Even the wood-burning stove, which the former owner had installed instead of the central heating the women would have preferred, burned efficiently all day and all night so that everyone was warm and snug. On the occasions when it was necessary to put on an extra sweater, it was no worse than in the days of his childhood, Joe insisted, to the derisory asides of his children about turn-of-the-previous-century man.

Downstairs the rooms of Ty Mawr opened out from each other. The bedrooms opened off a corridor and faced towards the Black Mountains, giving a breathtaking view of the changing seasons. There were rooms for privacy for the adults, who had gone to visit the house without the children to decide just how the living arrangements would work.

'If we have a matrimonial bed in each room,' Joe had suggested, 'there will be no problem of who sleeps where.'

'A winter woman and a summer woman,' interrupted Amanda wickedly.

It was too new; too delicate a subject for pleasantry. Sara

froze and even Joe looked a bit stern.

'I love you, Joe,' Amanda declared, 'but isn't it lucky you've got someone with a sense of humour.'

Sara had come to the same conclusion. She had always supposed that the reason for Joe's sexual prowess was his celibacy during the week. It was interesting to discover that here was a man with formidable needs.

'Amanda's right. It's not the sort of thing that should be left to chance, sharing your favours, no matter how embarrassed you may feel about it,' she said to him. 'And if you were going to suggest turn and turn about, that isn't at all a good idea, either.'

'A weekly rota?' he suggested humbly.

'We get the right of veto, though,' said Sara.

'Absolutely,' agreed Amanda.

'For example, I'm not a ball of fire at the moment, and we all know how Joe hated disturbed nights when the babies were tiny.'

'I remember,' Amanda said. 'But I also remember how comforting it is when you're pregnant to have a warm husband at your back. And there are the birthdays, and the days when you particularly want a cuddle,' she said generously.

'I don't think it will always be a question of ingenuity,' said Joe quietly. 'Do you?'

Sara went into labour on New Year's Eve. Joe said it was an omen for the future as he helped her into the car to drive her to the hospital in Abergavenny. Her fourth child, Joe's fifth, a girl whom they called Miriam, was born at 5.15 on New Year's morning. On account of the holiday, Sara was offered a lengthier stay than usual and, remembering the chaos still remaining at Ty Mawr, she agreed thankfully, whereupon the gynaecologist offered to tie her tubes for her. She accepted at once. Joe was a bit put out when she told him.

'Isn't five enough for you!' she exclaimed, her voice a little shrill so that the other visitors to the ward turned round to stare.

'Ssh!' hissed Joe, reddening. 'Yes. Yes, of course you're right,' he agreed hurriedly, if a trifle doubtfully.

'Believe me, I am.'

Ty Mawr welcomed the new arrival rapturously and after a few weeks it was as if the house had given itself a mental shake which set everything to rights. There seemed nothing, no ambitions, no desires that could not be explored within its framework.

Dareth arrived bearing a kitten, telling them that they'd need one for that house.

'Rats,' was what he told Joe succinctly. 'Them last lot wouldn't listen to me.' Dareth lived just down the road.

Joe translated this to: 'Dareth thinks we might need a cat for the occasional fieldmouse. He's also on the look out for a puppy.'

'A puppy!' From then on, Nicola was his devoted slave.

'Every house needs a dog.'

'Provided you walk it, Joe.' Amanda was a cat person.

'Good exercise. Davey and I'll do it together, won't we, son?'

Sara talked to Dareth over a piece of cake and learned that the lad had left school without any qualifications and had yet to find a job.

'Would you continue to work for us?' she asked casually.

'Yes,' came the eager reply. His mother had left the family three years previously and his father, unable to accept what had happened, had slid slowly into depression. Dareth said he would not leave him but he found the atmosphere barely tolerable. Working at Ty Mawr – and bringing home a wage, small though it was, gave him the necessary respite he needed. Having an outsider among the extended Williams family also served to give the situation a semblance of normality.

Harriet and Nicola were sharing one of the large bedrooms. Harriet regarded the move with more than mixed feelings. Though she found she was enjoying her A level course in design and business studies – her summer results being better than she had feared, though by no means as spectacular as Simon's had been – she had left behind many friends (and some of them were no loss, were Sara's caustic comments). But Ty Mawr and the unfamiliar people in it were a source of fascination which did a lot to ease her first few weeks until new friends were forthcoming.

'It's a pity Simon has missed most of the recent excitement,' Sara said to her daughter. Simon's required points had got him entry to York, his first-choice university. He had also opted to go back there immediately after Christmas, missing his half-sister's birth, but saying that he had an evening bar job which he didn't want to lose.

'I think Simon's a bit embarrassed by us,' commented Harriet shrewdly.

'Simon? Surely not,' Sara said, before she thought. Later she thought that if there was embarrassment it was more likely on account of herself. Sara was one of those who knew what had happened between Simon and Harriet. It was no wonder he felt uncomfortable in the presence of them all. Sometimes she wondered why she had still not mentioned that incident to her daughter. Then gradually it had come to her that discussing the birds and the bees angle was too late anyway. Well, naturally she had done that, before Harriet reached puberty, and she had given her carefully chosen books on the subject. Now she recognized something that should have been clear to her before, that her daughter was no longer uninitiated. Talking about being absolutely sure you wanted sex with a boy/man before you let him touch you seemed impossible in the light of the Simon episode.

Essentially I am a coward, Sara considered. *Just in the*

same way I was with Joe – or else I would have challenged him years ago about our way of life. If Harriet wants to talk about it, she will.

'Well, you know . . . I mean, we are a bit different.'

'As long as you don't feel the same way.' Was this the moment? Apparently it was not.

'My friends think we're, like, cool,' Harriet answered in the tone of voice that suggested she was not averse to the accolade.

'That's all right, then,' said Sara, hiding a relieved smile in Miriam's sweet-smelling hair.

It was the afternoon of Easter Sunday. Joe, replete from their roast lamb dinner followed by a truly delicious treacle tart which Aunt Ethel had provided, was finishing the papers. The children had stopped arguing over who had consumed the most Easter eggs and were now playing in the sunshine in the garden, their shrill voices muted by the distance. It was all peace, all harmony.

Not quite: Amanda and Sara, together on the large chintz-covered sofa, had had their heads together for some minutes. Joe rustled his paper once, twice. There was no response. He pushed the little cat off his lap, put his paper down and raised an eyebrow.

'All right. So what is it?' he asked.

The women regarded him, looked at each other. Sara nodded.

'We want to talk to you, Joe.'

'Fine, fine,' he said uneasily, looking at his watch. 'Haven't walked Dangermouse yet.' Dareth had come up with a three-year-old rescue mongrel who was proving a more efficient ratter than Sprig, the kitten. Davey, who had gained the animal's trust and affection at their first meeting had called him that and they were inseparable.

142

'Joe,' Sara protested, 'there's plenty of time before tea. David is playing with Dangermouse in the garden.'

'I suppose he is. Yes, of course there's time for a talk, though I wouldn't want to miss the simnel-cake you baked. It looks really rich.'

'And decorated by Harriet.'

'Beautifully decorated by Harriet.' Joe left his seat by the fireplace and they made room for him between them. 'I've been expecting something like this for some days. So who is going to tell me all about it?' he asked, running a gentle finger down Sara's cheek to her jawbone. Always a demonstrative man, Joe had at first been inhibited by the presence of another woman, but not for long.

Sara was surprised how little she minded Joe being demonstrative towards her with Amanda present, and also how little she minded when he was openly affectionate towards Amanda. She leant into his caress briefly.

'It's time we got on with developing the garden,' she said.

'I thought you'd done all the necessary digging. And weren't you telling us this morning that Dareth put in the potatoes on Shrove Tuesday to force just so we'd have new ones today?'

'I don't mean the planting. Perhaps I should have said expanding it. Chickens first, I thought. Then, maybe a goat.'

His face a study, Joe scrambled to his feet.

'We never set out to run a farm, you know. First there was Sprig, then Dangermouse, I suppose it'll be a cow after that, or a horse and cart.'

'Now that isn't a bad idea. Think of all that manure for the roses. . . .' Then Sara chuckled, taking pity on her over-wrought husband. 'Not a farm, dear, just a few free-range eggs.'

'Joe, don't be unreasonable,' Amanda said, her voice conciliatory. 'You were the one to turn our lives upside down. You have to expect changes, too, now that we are more settled. Yes,

I know. I started it,' she went on before he could intervene.

'And a great success that's been,' said Sara.

'I remember you warned me about this in the beginning,' said Joe. 'Though you led me to believe you'd be content with setting the garden to rights.'

'I've scarcely started that.'

'Which is what I mean. If you can't manage the garden, how come you are wanting to expand into animals?'

'Of course I can manage the garden. It's a question of the best use of what land we have,' said Sara. 'Like things happening at the right time. For instance, the trees in the orchard need pruning, but we missed the season for that so it'll have to wait until next winter. Then you'll see the crop we get. And I'll still have Dareth.' Dareth was a gem. 'He said it would be no problem for him to mend the ancient fruit-cage which will protect the raspberry and blackcurrant bushes. There's a gooseberry there, too.' Dareth had also started to wheedle for a small cultivator to go with the ride-on mower which Joe had already promised, but Sara thought she'd keep that for another day. 'Dareth is all for us selling our surplus vegetables.' (And growing more so that they would have a surplus, if she read him right.)

'If you say so,' Joe said uneasily. 'As for the other, what if you get too tired? You've still got the little ones to consider.'

'Miriam loves the outdoors. Yes, Joe, and I watch her. Very carefully.' There was a neighbour, a Mrs Lewis, who was a mine of knowledge when it came to gardening. She had become very fond of Miriam and was always ready to baby-sit when Sara needed her.

Sara was feeling better than she had in years, more energetic, more alive. She glanced across at Amanda who, she noticed, was the one looking more than a bit tired. Scarcely surprising, she supposed. She wouldn't have wanted to embark on an academic course, at any time. Of course, it could be just the change in their way of life (an early menopause, she wondered?).

'If it gets too much, or if it doesn't work out for either of us, we'll think again. After all, it's not as though we're asking you to buy more land.'

'More land? I should think not—'

'He's got that gleam in his eyes,' said Amanda. 'You know, the one—'

'That he gets when there's a new scheme in his mind?'

'That one.'

'Do you have to discuss me as though I'm not here?'

Sara laughed. 'Don't worry, love. Ty Mawr's three acres is probably all we'll ever want.'

'We love it here,' Amanda told him. 'You know that. I admit I was the one with the doubts, in spite of the idea being mine originally. But you're the one who made it all possible. Don't cramp us now, dear.' She gave Sara a significant nod. 'Tea, simnel-cake?' she suggested.

'I'll get it,' Sara said. 'Call the children in, will you, Joe?'

Joe waylaid Sara shortly afterwards.

'Are you truly happy about this outdoor work?' he asked her.

'Of course I am. Joe, you can't imagine how cramped I felt in that other house with a pocket-handkerchief for a veggie garden.'

'I thought it was charming, Georgian and all its roses and such.'

'Now you're hurt. It was just what we needed at the time. But things are different. The family is bigger. I have more time to do what I want. And I want this. Very much. It'll all be organic, too.'

'Well, I know how you feel about that.' He smiled.

'Even though you don't agree?'

'That's not true. I can see that knowing exactly what you

145

are putting into your children's mouths is extremely important nowadays. It's just the hard work of it.' He put his arms round her, cuddling her against him. 'You know how much I relied on you before we moved. In fact,' he said, 'I had wondered if you wouldn't want to work for me again, when you had more time.'

'Full-time? You mean go back to work in your office?'

'Well. Probably not in the office.'

'It wouldn't do, love,' she said gently, understanding just how Joe hated change, of any sort. 'And those arrangements you made when we moved. You could hardly alter them so soon.'

Joe had advertised for a home typist living not too far from Ty Mawr. He had found a woman in the village who was willing to do the work Sara had previously done.

'Well,' said Joe, a little vaguely, 'Mrs Thing says she is finding it a bit more tying than she'd intended.'

'Then I'm sure you'd find someone else, if you looked,' Sara replied reassuringly, as she ran her fingers through the hair at the base of Joe's neck. Joe's work – or at least the work he used to bring home for her – had never been more than a duty she felt she owed him to save them money. It was definitely not for her on a long-term basis. The house and the garden, all her wonderful plans, now that was different. 'There are lots of adverts for that sort of thing in the local paper,' she said, with a fine disregard for exactitude. 'You do understand, don't you.' She smiled winningly.

None of the children was about, so he gave her a long, satisfying kiss to show that he did – even if he didn't.

'So long as it's what you want,' he said at last, heavily.

'It is, dear. Absolutely.'

Chapter Fourteen

Amanda

You never knew what was going to happen to you. You had simply no idea how one minute you could be spending your time in a way that was totally predictable and the next life had thrown at you such shattering experiences that you felt as though you were drowning in a murky sea with no one caring to throw you the thinnest of ropes.

Sleep had become difficult and most nights nowadays Amanda found herself wakeful. Though she tried very hard to calm it, her mind fixed itself inexorably on those things over which she had no control. There was a time when her existence was humdrum; when she looked after a house and teenage son, went to a job in the local primary school, had a part-time husband, whom she loved dearly but who was only there at the weekends.

Joe. That had been the start of it all, that moment of unspeakable revelation when she discovered that she shared her husband with a personable (and actually very nice) younger woman, that her son had a half-brother and two half-sisters. Even more devastatingly, that there was to be yet another baby of Joe's. She had conceived only the once. There was a time when she yearned for another baby but, remembering Joe's reaction to the tiny Simon, she told herself she was lucky to have him. Anyway, it was obvious her fertility was low to non-existent as they had never taken any precautions. Was she envious of Sara? On balance, Amanda discovered she was not.

Then there was the move, an upheaval that was twice as cataclysmic as most people's moves because it involved openly sharing her life and her home with another family: Joe's other family. The morning after she and Simon arrived home after the canal holiday, Amanda stood in the middle of her small, immaculately tidy sitting-room and said fiercely to herself, *this is my home.*

How could she be expected to give it all up on a whim? Never mind that she, herself, was the originator of the whim. Amanda had suggested the move expecting both Joe and Sara to laugh at her. In the sanctuary of her own home she could see only the negative aspects of the idea: a house full of small children who were noisy and untidy. She would share Joe with another woman who would be demanding, bossy, a constant presence. It was too much to expect of any woman.

She thought she actually hated Joe for agreeing so eagerly, so quickly.

That coming upheaval was compounded by another total life change; from being a very minor cog in a primary school, in less than a year Amanda was to become a student at a college campus which would naturally teem with the young. She was not sure which was going to be the more formidable, the academic work or the new world in which it would place her. She had only ever contemplated the venture as an impossible fantasy and she was amazed at how easily she had succumbed to Sara's blandishments about her capabilities. Her mind reeled with the sheer audacity of it. Yet it was real and it began to happen almost as soon as the holiday was over.

Without too much difficulty Amanda found a retired maths teacher who was happy to initiate her into A Level maths. Except that to his relief — and to her own astonishment — there were few intricacies. She relished the challenge of the subject, its discipline, its beauty once she recognized its formalities. He assured her, and she was more than willing to believe, that once her college work started she would certainly not be flagging behind the others.

'Doing the work in one year will mean you won't have time to be bored,' he told her, thinking privately what a waste all these years had been for her.'

So life was hectic. Once she was home (where now Joe was all the time), there were the inevitable chores. It was true there was another woman, but you could not expect a new mother to want to spend too much time on housework, nor would Amanda have wanted to abandon her home to another woman. There were machines for washing clothes, hoovering the carpets, washing the dishes, but someone had to tend those machines and it was still hard work. It was interesting to notice that, released from many of the inside jobs, and once her strength had fully returned, Sara particularly enjoyed working outside — which Amanda had never done. The fresh air was obviously good for Sara, and Miriam thrived, becoming very quickly a brown bundle of chuckles, adored as she was by everyone.

Often Amanda shook herself mentally, telling herself sternly not to whinge. Most of these life-changes of hers were positive, and positively good. Ty Mawr was good for Harriet, she noticed. In the back of her mind, Amanda felt somehow responsible for Harriet's well-being on account of the mess her son had almost made of the girl's life.

She had decided to confront Simon about that incident on holiday before he went to university. There was something she needed to clarify while he was still with them – though her motherly instincts knew that he had escaped her already, if maybe not for ever.

'That time on the canal when we first found out about your father. Did you, with Harriet? You know what I mean?'

Not sufficiently worldly-wise to prevaricate – or perhaps he just wanted to reassure her with the truth, Simon answered:

'No. Mum. Mind you, it was a close-run thing.'

'Brat.'

'And not my fault if it had happened.'

'Nor Harriet's.'

'Definitely not Harriet's. It was bad of Dad, wasn't it, keeping us from each other? What if . . . I mean . . .'

He did not say the sex would have been unprotected. She thought the time was not right to sermonize.

'It was very wrong,' she agreed soberly. 'You won't let it spoil your relationship with your father, will you, though?'

He shrugged. 'Whatever. I guess that's up to him.'

It was inevitable that Simon should drift from them, though it saddened her immeasurably. Perhaps Amanda worried more about it than Joe,who said that it was only to be expected once a young man left home.

'He'll be back, you'll see.'

In the meantime, Amanda comforted herself by sending regular e-mails in which she concentrated on telling him about her own work (even asking occasionally for his advice) and relating the more impersonal details about the rest of the family, for she knew he did not correspond with his father. Every so often Simon actually replied to her e-mails, so she felt that the links between them, though stretched, were still intact.

It amazed Amanda that she could not only have suggested sharing her husband with another woman but that the scheme could work. Of course it could only have come about as a result of the way she and Joe had lived for so many years.

Part-time. If they had been a normal couple there was no doubt in her mind that she would have left him the moment she learnt the truth about Sara. Living with Joe as she had, learning to stand away from their relationship and appreciate it for what it was, had given her perspective enough to accept openly what it had now become.

It amazed her even more that the resentment she had felt, what could have become hatred of Joe if she had not known how destructive it would be to her own well-being, had gone. She still loved him, still admitted him to her bed (and continued to enjoy extremely satisfactory sex with him).

It helped that she really liked Sara.

Looking in her mirror she sometimes wondered whether this was another example of a man taking as his mistress someone who resembled his wife, for they had the same colouring, the same dark hair, worn almost identically. Except that occasionally she saw signs of ageing that were not apparent in Sara; lines and a certain sagging of the flesh.

There was another matter that currently perturbed her. All her life Amanda had enjoyed good health. She had suffered the usual childish complaints, mildly. She had recovered completely from childbirth. She never had headaches (by whatever name), rarely caught a cold and was still miraculously free from joint pains from which all too many of her women friends were beginning to complain.

But for some months now there had been bouts of tiredness, which probably explained the lines, she told herself. She treated herself to an expensive pot of cream and hoped they would go away. Wasn't she worth it? She smiled at her reflection and thought her skin looked firmer already, though, *What do you expect, woman*, she chided herself? Such a total turnaround of her life was bound to affect her somehow. All that brainwork was taking it out of her. It had been so many years since she had read a non-fiction book. The French, which she was developing with a correspondence course, was particularly demanding. The vocabulary wasn't a problem, it was the grammar. She did so hope it would become easier once she got to college.

Then a few weeks later, Amanda had been filling the front-loading washing-machine when she was aware of a peculiar sensation in her left breast. It almost felt as though a pump was filling it, as though in an extraordinary way she was a balloon. One moment, nothing; the next – she felt it gingerly – there was a lump. She stopped what she was doing and felt it again. She had not imagined it. The lump was there, slightly to the left of her nipple, nearer the bottom of the breast than the top. Definitely there.

Amanda continued loading the washing-machine. She put Sara's chicken casserole in the oven. She made an apple tart. She did not touch herself again. In bed – Joe was in the other room with Sara – Amanda, once more carefully avoided touching herself, turned on to her right side for sleep, which for once came almost immediately. In the morning, as she was putting on her bra, Amanda's hand brushed against her breast. The lump was still there.

It'll go away. These things probably happen all the time to women of my age. It's nothing.

She told no one. What was there to tell? She wasn't going to any doctor. The lump was nothing, really, neither large nor hard. It was certainly not getting any bigger – which would have alarmed her. She'd heard of women who had breast cysts. Didn't they just dry up eventually? Then, what would she say to the doctor? You couldn't say you just felt tired. That was pathetic, besides, what was the woman supposed to do, give you a pill? Though it was plain even to the least observant that she was tired, for her skin had become sallow again and her hair, which she was wearing drawn off her face, was lank. Perhaps it was an early menopause, Amanda thought, her heart sinking. She remembered her mother all too well, a woman who had never really recovered from her change of life, either physically or mentally. Her own periods were still like clockwork.

That afternoon, quite by chance, one of the staff started talking about alternative cures. She had a book, the teacher said, a compendium of the various disasters that befell the human race, particularly the female half of it. At the end of the day Amanda waited for her to leave.

'That book you mentioned this morning.'

'Which one? Oh, my alternative cures. Would you like to borrow it?'

She brought it in the next day and in bed that night Amanda skimmed through the pages on breast cancer. (Not that she had cancer.) It seemed to offer sensible advice. She read it more carefully. It seemed that there were simple changes she might make to her life that would be beneficial, like cutting out red meat and dairy products. That wouldn't be too difficult. Joe liked his beef but Amanda had never cooked very much of it because of the cost, mainly bringing the children up on fish and chicken. It was helpful that Sara preferred to follow much the same regime. Amanda would miss the cheeses but they now had milk from their two goats and their own eggs. She thought that any changes she made would hardly be noticed — certainly not when compared with Harriet's recent diet which though not vegan, forbade all meat, fish and eggs. Alcohol. Mm . . . Well, thought Amanda, she'd always said she should cut down on the wine and as she'd never smoked, that was one bonus.

Afterwards Amanda realized that if she had been living alone with Joe she could probably have concealed her lump for ever — even though the book said that sex was good for you and Joe was nothing if not good with his hands. Living with Sara was another matter.

They were in the sitting-room together on another Sunday afternoon; Joe was in the garden with Nicola and David, Miriam was playing quietly at their feet. 'When are you going to start taking a tonic?' Sara asked abruptly.

'I don't need a tonic. Who says I do?'

'Me. You've been tired on and off for weeks.'

'You've not said anything before.'

'I thought you'd prefer to discuss it with Joe, maybe go and see your GP.'

Amanda shrugged. 'It's nothing.'

'Is it all your bookwork?'

'No. Certainly not. I love all of it.'

'Even the French. Come on, I've heard you complain about that.'

'I promise you, even that.'

'Then what is it, Amanda? There must be something. Look.' Sara pulled her gently to her feet and turned her towards the mirror hanging over the mantelpiece. 'You don't eat, at least you eat less than Harriet. You've dark circles under your eyes, lank hair, and the only reason your eyes are sparkling now is because you're angry. This has been going on for too long. Either you tell me now what the matter is, or I tell Joe to fix it.'

'I don't think this is anything Joe can fix.'

'Then who can?'

There was a moment's pause. Sara turned away. As she reached the door Amanda said quietly:

'I have a lump in my breast. It won't go away.'

Sara's intake of breath was startling in that quiet room.

'Oh, Amanda. When did you discover it? Today, yesterday?'

Amanda laughed. 'You're joking? Today?'

'If I ever find a breast lump, I'm in that surgery the next day, at the very latest. So, what does the doctor say? What are they doing about it?'

154

'I've not been to the doctor.'

'Not had time? You mustn't waste time. You know that. Hang on, you've been looking tired for ages. Just when did you discover the lump?'

'Two months ago.'

Sara's jaw sagged visibly. 'I don't believe . . . No, no one jokes about a thing like that. Amanda, what in hell's name were you doing, neglecting yourself. . . .'

'I haven't been neglecting myself,' Amanda answered hotly. 'I've been very careful with my diet. I've given up red meat, dairy products and alcohol. I've—'

'Gone for alternative cures without seeing your doctor. I thought you, of all people, would have had more sense.'

'How dare you!'

'Hey, what's going on? Sara, Amanda? What's the row about?'

'You tell him,' said Sara, pushing past Joe. 'He has to know and you have to do something about it. Tomorrow.'

Amanda was beginning to weep. Joe took her into his arms.

'Hey. It must be something awful, if you need to cry about it? Have I done something wrong?'

'Oh, Joe, do you constantly feel guilty about things, nowadays? You never used to apologize before without knowing what you'd done.' Amanda sniffed. 'Give us your hankie.'

Joe complied. Then: 'Just a minute,' he said. 'I think I've been distracted. Why were you crying.'

'No reason. I'm just a bit tired.'

'Anyone can see that,' said Joe, who had just realized it was all too true. 'Why are you tired?' he persisted.

Amanda crumpled, sinking on to the sofa.

'I have a breast lump.'

'Oh. They can do wonders for breast cancer now, can't they.'

Amanda wailed, 'I haven't got breast cancer.'

'Then what—'

'But she doesn't actually know. Either way,' said Sara, who had decided to linger at the door, whatever the house rules were when Joe was talking to one of his women. 'Do you, Amanda?'

Amanda shook her head mutely.

'Idiot,' said Joe fondly, unaware as yet how long this foolishness had been maintained.

'We shall go to the doctor tomorrow, shan't we, Amanda?'

Amanda sighed. 'I'm not a child.' She saw Joe and Sara exchange a meaningful glance and didn't know whether to laugh or cry. It was such a ridiculous situation. But it was also such a relief to have the decisions taken from her. In the end she both laughed and wept, and the comforting almost made up for all the months of strain that had gone before so that Amanda no longer cared how they saw her, child or idiot.

There followed a period of extreme stress. It was Sara who picked up the telephone on the Monday morning to ask for an immediate appointment, which, as luck would have it, was with Amanda's own doctor. It was Sara who insisted on accompanying her to the surgery.

'I am perfectly capable of going on my own.'

'Of course you are. I thought you might like the company. Unless Joe . . .'

'I am meeting a client,' Joe said hurriedly. There was a pause. 'But if you really need me . . .'

Amanda sighed inwardly. 'It's all right, Joe. If Sara can come . . .'

'I'll need to bring Miriam, but I don't expect you would want me to come into the doctor's room with you?'

Amanda shook her head. It was probably just as well Joe couldn't come. Having him there, sitting beside her in the waiting-room was one thing. Waiting for him to interrogate the doctor on her behalf, demand explanations as to the whys and whens when all she really wanted was for the thing to go away (be taken away?) could be too much of a good thing.

'Thank you,' she said.

Her GP, a sensible and kindly woman of about her own age, did not even chide her.

'You'll need to be seen as a matter of urgency. It could be one of two things, a cyst or a tumour. If it's a cyst there's most likely nothing to worry about. These happen.'

'If it's a tumour?'

'It's either benign, and harmless, or, worst-case scenario, malignant.'

'What happens then?'

'Shall we just wait and see?'

The appointment at the breast clinic in Cardiff was twelve days after Amanda had first seen the doctor. Once again Sara came with her. This time they left Miriam at home with Mrs Lewis. She had sold them their first twelve laying Rhode Island hybrids — which were guaranteed good layers and easy to breed — and she insisted on keeping what she called a motherly eye on their little flock. Without the least display of curiosity she immediately agreed to look after the baby when Sara explained that Amanda had a hospital appointment.

Amanda had been warned the proceedings would take most of the morning. She might, or might not, be given a diagnosis before she left.

'If you are in the clear we'll go and have some lunch, then cheer ourselves up in Howells. Buy you a dress.'

'Fat lot of good a dress'll be to me.'

'Oh, I don't know. You could look for something ready for autumn. I expect the other students wear smart things sometimes.'

Amanda managed a small smile.

'Jeans and baggy tops.'

'I saw some pretty camisole tops for the summer in a magazine.' Sara realized what she had said immediately. 'Sorry, sorry.'

'I'm just going to have to get used to it, aren't I?'

'But if you are in the clear, a camisole top would be the icing on the cake, now wouldn't it? Think what Joe would say.'

Amanda was more concerned with what Joe's reaction would be when he discovered she was about to lose her breast.

'Don't give it a moment's thought,' warned Sara.

'All right. Lunch, then shopping,' agreed Amanda.

There was a triple assessment. First came a breast examination, very similar to the one her GP had given her. 'It's a good thing you went to your doctor,' the consultant said – also without telling her she had been stupid to delay her visit. 'I'll see you later on, mm?'

As she was over thirty-five, Amanda had a mammogram rather than an ultrasound scan. She thought the mammogram was one of the most uncomfortable proceedings devised by man, when both her breasts were squashed flat by an x-ray machine.

'You are very good,' said the technician soothingly, 'some of our ladies don't half make a fuss.' If anything that made her feel worse. After all, it hadn't really hurt, the plate had just been tight for a minute.

Last of all there was a fine-needle aspiration cytology which, logically, they called a FNAC. This drew off cells using a fine needle and syringe.

Her appointment had been early. 'We should have your results by mid-afternoon,' she was told. 'Come back at three o'clock.'

'That means lunch,' said Sara. 'Good. I'm starving.'

'I don't think I want to go anywhere near the city centre after all,' said Amanda. 'Could we use the canteen?'

'Sure. Then we'll get some fresh air.'

*

The consultant sat her down solicitously, so that she had the feeling something was wrong before he began.

'Mrs Williams, we found a few malignant cells, I'm afraid. It means surgery. . . .'

'In a couple of weeks, he told me,' Amanda explained to Joe that evening. 'I'm not going to lose my breast,' she said emphatically – feeling sure this was important. 'He said it's small enough for a lumpectomy to remove the tumour with an area of healthy tissue around it. But even with the – the delay, the prognosis is good.'

Joe had gone pale. 'I mean, hell, that's bad enough, but you've not mentioned therapy, you know . . .'

'The sort where I lose my hair?' A faint smile crossed her face. 'Yup. I guess the chemotherapy'll make me feel sick and the radiotherapy will make my hair fall out – or is it the other way round? Whatever, as Harriet would say.'

'How can you joke about it?'

'How not? What would be the point of weeping and gnashing my teeth? If it happens, it happens. And I've always loved hats. Besides, the chances of a total recovery are very high nowadays.'

She did not say that a percentage of women had a reoccurrence of the cancer – and that of those some still made a total recovery. There was no point in overloading the family with depression. Positive. She had to think positively. Be positive. She'd take the therapies and she'd adopt a lifestyle that was designed to preserve her mental and physical wellbeing, as well as continuing with her studies. After all, if she was one of the lucky ones, she'd need the stimulation of intellectual exercise as well as the physical part. (And if she wasn't, she'd need it even more.) She thought that if she'd been a praying woman she'd probably go to church. But she never had been, not believing in a god with whom she had an intimate, daily, relationship. She just had to do it the hard way.

'But, hey, though we're right to be anxious, it is good news.' Once again Sara took the initiative, became the commonsensical one. 'That's good, Joe, isn't it? Really great.'

They had managed to keep things from Harriet until the time came when Amanda went into hospital. So they thought.

'Gross,' said Harriet to Amanda after her mother had told her. 'As in, I mean, not a cool thing to happen,' she said hurriedly.

'I couldn't help it,' Amanda said defensively.

'I knew there was something wrong. I just wondered if you couldn't hack the coursework because you're a bit old, and that was why you were looking so haggard.'

'Harriet!'

'Sorry. Will you get sick and lose your hair?'

'I'm not sure, yet.'

'Because there's a shop in Cardiff with these great hats. Um, if you ever need one, that is. Cool colours, too.'

'That would be very kind,' said Amanda shakily.

'We couldn't help noticing, you see.'

'I suppose not. Has Simon been concerned, too, do you know?'

'I e-mailed him ages ago. He thought you might be going through the change, so I stopped worrying.'

Amanda made a helpless gesture.

'I wonder why we didn't give you both the benefit of adult feelings?'

'Whatever.'

Chapter Fifteen

Joe on Joe

All in all it was quite a summer. Now I'm not going to excuse myself for not discovering about Amanda before I was told. She was nothing if not capable of keeping a secret, as Sara and I found out when it could have been too late. I like to think I was truly supportive, but when Amanda came home from her treatments feeling nauseous and very tired it was obviously to Sara to whom she turned. Sara was a star. To tell the truth I'm a bit out of my depth with people who are unwell. I never know what to say. Clumsy, Harriet calls it. It doesn't mean that I didn't care. Amanda knew that and I couldn't get over how marvellous she was through it all and fortunately the sickness only affected her for a short time.

The only bad time was when her hair first began to fall out. It was the one time I saw her cry except for that time she told us about the cancer, and then it was Harriet who came to the rescue by bringing home an absurd hat which made Amanda laugh, and after that it was all right. You know, a bald woman can look amazingly sexy, especially if she has strong cheekbones. Amanda had lost quite a bit of weight and the structure of her face stood out. I was so proud of her. I was proud of us all, individually and as a family.

So why didn't these feelings persist?

There was this afternoon during the following summer. I'd found myself with time to spare. I decided to go home early. They were in the garden, Amanda and Sara, Davey, Nicola and Miriam, having tea on a rug under the apple tree. I couldn't explain it, but approaching the group I suddenly felt excluded, redundant.

I realized it was not the first time. Somehow the feeling that I was in control of my life had gone. Amanda, now at uni (the University of Wales's Newport campus – of course she got there, she passed all her exams and she was accepted readily and doing very well, by all accounts), Sara with the garden, both appeared too busy to pay me much attention unless I asked for it. That, as you know is not something a man likes to demand. He expects it. Admittedly life had been fraught, in the old days. Now it seemed to me that there was not even spontaneity any more. Life was tranquil; life was dull!

I'd been hovering at the edge of the rug for a minute or so before anyone noticed me. I saw the women exchange glances.

'Back early Joe?' Amanda said cautiously.

'Daddy. Daddy.' Nicola leapt for my arms. Bless her, you could always count on Nicola. 'Do you know what Miriam did today?'

'Tell me, pet.'

'She walked six steps.' Miriam had chattered away since she was twelve months old. She crawled very fast but the art of walking was taking a little longer.

'Do you think she'd do it again, for me?'

'I don't know. Why don't you ask her? She might walk for you, though I think she's too interested in her chocky bikky.'

'Tea, Joe?'

I got down on the rug and took the cup from Amanda.

'How come you've no work, or are you on your way somewhere?'

'Everything seems to be under control. I thought I'd have an hour or so off, for a change.'

'That's nice.'

I grinned at Amanda and she grinned back.

'It's the second time this week. Why don't you give yourself a holiday? A proper holiday. Maybe do some walking in the Black Mountains.'

Holidays had always been a bit fraught. I guess you know that. None of us had taken a holiday since we'd all met up on the canal.

'By myself?' I shook my head automatically, thought better of it. 'Oh, I don't know . . .' Despite myself I began to plan it mentally. 'You said you wanted help with some fencing at the end of the week,' I said reluctantly.

'That would still give you five days,' said Sara.

'Mm. You know, that's not a bad idea. Anyone any idea where I put my boots?'

'If they're not with all the wellies by the back door, or in the garden shed, you've probably left them at Aunt Ethel's,' said Amanda.

'Come to think of it,' said Sara, 'haven't you been neglecting her recently? I can't remember when you last relayed messages from her and we haven't had one of her delicious treacle tarts or a fruit-cake for weeks. Is Aunt Ethel all right?'

'How could we all have forgotten about Aunt Ethel!'

The question was totally unexpected. I swallowed, hastily produced a handkerchief and blew my nose vigorously. Aunt Ethel! Panic flooded me. When was I last supposed to have seen her? What had I told them? *Calm down, calm down*, my inner voice urged. *Don't blow it now.*

'Didn't I tell you?' I began. 'No,' I answered myself. 'I decided not to worry you.'

'Joe!' exclaimed Amanda.

'She's not ill?' asked Sara anxiously.

'No. No. As a matter of fact we had a slight row. Well, a humdinger of a row, if you want the truth,' I said, embroidering elaborately. 'About the new accountant. I told you about him?' When both women shook their heads, I tut-tutted, 'There you are. So much has happened recently.' I shrugged. 'Anyway, I decided to stay away for a week or so. Just to let the dust settle.'

'Joe, that's unlike you,' Amanda said reproachfully. 'Holding a grudge. I think you should forget about the walking and go and see her instead.'

'Maybe one of us should come with you?' suggested Sara. 'Mightn't it help clear the air?'

'She still doesn't know we all live together. But I expect you're right,' I said hastily. 'If you ask me, it's only a touch of senility. Nothing wrong with her health, mind. She just can't bear to let go and this time she's interfered once too often.'

'Nothing strange in that,' said Amanda gently.

But as Amanda had said, how could I have forgotten Aunt Ethel? It was definitely time to cultivate her again, senile or not, or wherever my boots were.

'That's settled, then,' I declared. 'This weekend I'll go walking and call in on Aunt Ethel on my way home.'

Chapter Sixteen

Simon

That summer was catastrophic.

Well, he supposed it hadn't turned out so badly by the time he arrived in York, but for a while there, Simon had felt so gutted he'd wondered whether anything would be worth while ever again.

Simon had always felt closer to his mother than to his father. That wasn't so surprising when you realized how little time Joe spent with his family. There were occasions when Simon deeply resented his father's absence from school concerts – though he knew that he was by no means the only kid with just one parent to support them. There were the odd instances when this was an advantage, like when there was that particularly messy session with the head – he'd been bunking off with a couple of friends and they'd been caught smoking in a shopping mall. He'd got away with a caution, and Amanda had been so grateful he'd not been doing drugs (as if), she'd torn him off a strip, but not told his father.

There were times when Joe turned up for cricket matches and got on easily with the other fathers. They were good times. But they didn't happen very often.

In many ways his uncle, John, had been more of a father

figure. It had been a blow when John married, especially since Fay could be a real pain if she thought she wasn't getting her own way. Honestly, how a man like John had fallen for a woman like Fay defeated him. But there you go.

His mother's suggestion that they should all go away together on a canal holiday – without his father's knowledge – had seemed such a lark. Why not? It was something to do during the holidays while he was waiting for his results.

The exams.

Simon knew he was blessed with a good brain. He had always intended going to uni. He'd toyed with various courses, but had decided eventually that economics would be interesting and, hopefully, vocational: i.e. it would lead to the sort of job that landed loads of dosh. His offer from York was ABB, which seemed very reasonable and entirely achievable. And so he continued to play the drums and . . . well, generally fool around, until suddenly there wasn't all that much time left. Simon was sufficiently level-headed, then, to channel all his energies exactly where they were needed. When he sat the exams they were do-able. He came out of the hall after each one feeling quite pleased with himself.

Then the reaction set in. There were night sweats, moments of total panic when all he could do was throw up. There was no one he could tell: John was too preoccupied, his mother would have been too worried. It didn't occur to him to consult a doctor. There had been one teacher, but he'd retired at the end of the summer term to go and live in Devon. Simon suffered on his own.

He'd had the usual run of girl friends, Lindy being the last. Surprisingly, Simon was still a virgin. (Sometimes it appalled him). But there hadn't been anyone who had done it for him, and once he became so neurotic about his exams even Lindy began to find excuses why they should cease to be an item.

Then he met Harriet. He knew it was testosterone. Yet

there was something about her that triggered a feeling that was unique. He'd never felt like that about any girl before. There was this way she tossed her head. There was a little habit she had of chewing her thumb. It made him go all soft inside. And they'd only known each other for a couple of days. It was absurd. He knew he was behaving worse than any nerd.

He remembered an afternoon in spring when he wanted something from his mother (a cash advance, probably) and she'd been watching *Neighbours* so he'd stood behind her chair with barely concealed impatience until the episode ended. Two of the younger characters had been at it and declaring themselves soul mates. He'd just stopped himself from sniggering (reasoning his mum wasn't going to be well-disposed if he ruined her soap). But surprisingly the idea of his soul mate out there, somewhere, stuck. He'd found himself wondering if Harriet was the one almost as soon as they'd met.

Then he found out – in the worst of all possible ways – that Harriet wasn't just any girl. She was his sister. Correction, his half-sister. It was fucking ridiculous. It was . . .

And his father had caught him fondling his sister.

His mother knew something had happened (though not exactly what – but she wasn't a fool).

Simon was furious with his father. He was enraged with himself because it looked as if any plans he'd made that would take him into an environment where no one knew of his past had been endangered by his stupid complacency. In other words, it was worse because it was all his own fault.

Strange that it was Harriet who had provided the one ray of hope with her positive attitude. He thought they could be real friends, as brother and sister. Half-brother and sister.

Looking back, the one thing he thought he'd done right was not letting Harriet know just how much he had fancied her.

Letting her think it had all been just a bit of fun that had gone a little bit pear-shaped had probably let her get over him the sooner. At least he thought it had. Not so very long after he'd gone away, it sounded as though she'd got a thing going with that local fellow called Dareth who was working for Sara. When he heard, he'd seethed, knowing Dareth wasn't good enough.

Now that was a thing. Not only did it appear that Joe had another family, he was setting up house with both women. There were moments when Simon felt almost proud of the old man's luck.

Then he remembered that one of the women was his mother and he burned with embarrassment.

So the results of his exams, which were better than he'd hoped and better even than predicted, got him away from Ty Mawr. He was to live in hall for the first year (which in one way was a bore but realistically cushioned his first months away from the mothering he'd come to rely on), but after that things would change. Simon had had a talk with his father. Was it guilt on Joe's part? Simon wasn't sure, but Joe had suggested that at the end of his first year they should invest in a small house with a couple of extra bedrooms which he could then rent out, the rent covering the mortgage and bills. Brilliant!

That first Christmas was made bearable because it was so short – though having the small children around did help. They'd even had stockings and had written letters to Santa. But he couldn't wait to get away, from his father, despite the generosity, from the atmosphere of congeniality (false? – he wasn't inclined to delve into the complexities if it were genuine). From Harriet. He'd pleaded a bar job – the job was a fact, but the urgency was faked. Easter passed in work – a necessity. He made a flying visit in the summer to collect a few things for the student house. Then he went abroad for a month with friends. Would he ever have returned to Ty Mawr? There were times when Simon wondered. But his mother became ill.

The cancer business was shit.

It was Harriet who began texting him, once Amanda had written to tell him – she usually e-mailed, so he knew it was serious.

In the middle of the awfulness there was a time when Simon was sure Amanda was going to die and it was so scary. There was one message that gave him hope:

☺ yr mum not 2 sick wants 2 buy hat [!] xOTC (which Simon knew meant kiss on the cheek). It was signed H.

Purposefully he went to the market where the clothes' stalls were. He found a velvet hat, a sort of purple and gold turban, and posted it to his mother. Amanda said she loved it, so for the next few weeks whenever Simon saw something on the same stall he bought it. He hoped his mother would be happy that he was thinking of her constantly.

There was a girl called Mary on the stall, doing Saturdays. It turned out she was also at the uni, in his year and reading psychology. She was curious about the hats and he found himself talking to her more easily than he had to anyone else, Harriet included. Mary was very sympathetic and started to keep back likely purchases when he'd explained, sheepishly – because he feared she might laugh – why he was interested. She was very pretty – a little like Harriet. They met up in the bar one evening when he was working and discovered that they both admired the saxophonist, Artie Shaw. Before long they were inseparable. Would he take her home? It was not impossible, Simon thought. Maybe one day.

Chapter Seventeen

Joe

Joe set off along the Offa's Dyke path outside Abergavenny. Above the town there were few people about and the peace and quiet of the ridge filled him with pleasure. The ground was flat and wide and overwalked in places, which had become wet and boggy, but shifting the backpack so that it sat more comfortably, he breathed deeply and began to whistle as he leapt boyishly from heather patch to heather patch, reminding himself not to do too much this first day, for already he knew he was a bit out of condition.

Above Llanthony Priory, its ruins brooding darkly in late afternoon shadow, Joe took the steep trail off the ridge to find his night's accommodation. Before he set off he had been to Abergavenny's tourist office where he settled for a farmhouse B&B. Down in the valley this B&B was unmistakable, with a 'vacancy' sign hanging outside and pots of geraniums by the front door. That the farmer's wife also offered an evening meal was an added bonus. Joe was delighted. It had all come just as his feet were beginning to hurt.

A large mug of tea and a bath later, Joe was feeling happier. The meat pie was succulent, the steamed pudding that followed it filling. A pint at the pub down the road, he decided, would just prepare him for bed.

In the pub he began talking to a group of walkers who were also staying nearby. There were five of them, three men and two girls. One of the girls had injured her knee and it looked as though she could not continue. Her boyfriend was not too upset, said they'd probably stay where they were for a few days. They'd go now, they said. It was time she was resting.

The second girl said her name was Tessa. A bit sullen, was Joe's instant reaction, not his type at all, though she was pretty enough in an obvious sort of way, with heavy breasts totally unsupported under a tight T-shirt and heavy fair hair falling over her face.

After a gin and tonic, which she got down with speed, Tessa confided to Joe that the accident was the last straw.

'My whole holiday's ruined. First it was my boyfriend who had to cancel. Mal said he'd got flu, or something. Now this. Who wants to be gooseberry with those two?' She indicated the other two men who were talking together, their heads close.

'Where were you going?'

'Just as far as we could, by Thursday. We're supposed to be on a budget. But no one but me seems to want to stick to it. So I might as well go home.'

'Don't do that,' Joe said impulsively.

'Why not?' There was a challenge in her young face.

Joe groaned, inwardly aghast by what he'd said. 'The weather's set fair,' he said lamely. 'Where do you come from, anyway?'

'Birmingham. Well, Cumbria, but I work in Birmingham. Can't you tell by the accent?' she asked mockingly. 'On your own, are you?'

'That's right.'

'But married?' When he nodded, she observed: 'Most men are. The nice ones, anyway.' She smiled, and Joe's loins stirred unexpectedly. Tessa scrutinized him, then she twisted her body gauchely. 'Were you wanting company on your walk tomorrow?'

Joe opened his mouth to say a firm *no*. After all, the whole point of this holiday was to get away from it all. It?

'I'm supposed to be having a couple of days getting some fresh air and exercise,' he admitted, 'but you can get a bit lonely after a few hours of your own company.'

'If I do decide not to go home tomorrow, I could do with some company, too. But you don't have to walk with me,' she added defensively.

Joe patted her hand in what he fondly imagined was an avuncular fashion. It was that last statement that decided him.

'Let's leave it until tomorrow, then. Your friend might have decided she can walk after all.'

'My friend is probably exactly where she wants to be, right now.' Tessa's meaning was crudely obvious. 'I bet she fell deliberately.'

Joe experienced a moment of shock, then he chuckled. The young were so much less hypocritical nowadays. Tessa wasn't his type at all, he decided, though he'd bet she'd be good company for a day or so.

'Let's leave it until tomorrow,' he repeated.

Tessa was already at Llanthony Priory's ruins at the appointed time. There they started the steep climb back to the ridge. Joe's spirits lifted. To begin with, neither talked much. She walked with an easy stride and he felt as if he could go on for miles once his initial stiffness wore off. Eventually they stopped for a break.

'What will your boyfriend say when he hears you've ditched your friends? Won't he mind?' asked Joe.

'Whatever do you mean?'

He sighed impatiently. No one could be that innocent.

'For heaven's sake, girl, I could be a rapist.'

'But you aren't.'

'Of course I'm not. But if I were your boyfriend—'

'Mal isn't. Any more. I ditched him. I was bored. Joe, I do hope you're not going to turn out to be a prig,' she said coldly. 'I trust my judgement. Now, if you'd made any suggestions last night, that would have been different.'

'What do you take me for? I told you, I'm married.'

'So you did. And you're here, without your wife. But I still trust you.'

Joe felt flattered. Whether he deserved to be was another matter.

At Hay Bluff they left the ridge and walked down into the town to look around. They bought provisions for the next day and Joe began to browse in the second-hand bookshops. Tessa became fidgety.

'All right,' Joe conceded, laughing. 'I couldn't carry much more, anyway. Let's see if the tourist information office can fix us up for the night.'

They returned to Offa's Dyke and later in the afternoon reached the small brick cottage where they were expected.

'I get rung up a lot this time of year,' the owner, an elderly woman, said. 'It's only the one room I have for couples, see, but I like a bit of company on a summer's night.'

Joe glanced surreptitiously at Tessa who was leaning against the porch, fiddling with the strap of her backpack.

'Williams, did you say the name is? Come on in, then.' The woman placed a guiding hand on Joe's arm. 'I dare say your wife would like a wash while I put the kettle on.'

The room was sunny but the large yellow cabbage-roses splashed over the wallpaper made it seem even smaller than it was, while the double bed, by contrast, loomed huge in the middle of the floor. Joe reminded himself that it was Tessa who had made the booking. He had been side-tracked into another bookshop. He leant against the door.

'What've you got us into?' he muttered. 'Had I better go and explain?'

'Explain what?'

'That we're not . . . That woman thinks we're married.'

'Of course she does. It's not easy finding two single rooms, you know. Besides, it's cheaper this way.'

'But we can't . . . I mean, you can't want . . . Both of us in that bed.'

'It looks very comfortable to me, and I'm sure as hell not going to start looking for anything else. I can't wait to get my boots off.' She wrenched at them, letting them fall to the floor with a small thud. Then she wriggled her toes pleasurably.

Joe was still uneasy. Of course they could sleep in a bed, together, without anything happening between them. But. . . . And suppose someone found out?

She was lying across the bed.

'Don't be stuffy, Joe,' she said. Then she said: 'Mm. It is comfortable.' Her eyes, staring at him, were pools of deep water which he could not fathom. 'It even sags in the right places.' She rolled away from him. 'I don't see any problem. If you do, that's up to you, isn't it.'

Tessa slept. Joe did not. What kind of a fool was he, he asked himself. Not just a fool who had allowed himself to drift into this situation, a crass idiot who seemed incapable of preventing himself from encouraging situations that were bound to go awry. The sensible thing was for the two of them to part company in the morning, he decided. He'd walk on his own, as he'd planned.

It was not as easy as that.

'I think, maybe, this won't work after all,' he began at breakfast. 'Maybe we shouldn't walk together, after all.'

'You what?' demanded an incredulous Tessa, helping

herself to more coffee. 'You ditching me in the wilds of Wales?'

Put like that, what could he say? 'I wouldn't leave you to walk alone,' Joe said quietly, 'but there'll be no more double beds, huh?'

She shrugged. 'If that's what you want.'

On the morning of his last day Joe asked Tessa what her plans were when they parted.

'How much longer are you on holiday?'

'I thought I'd stick with you until the last moment,' she answered.

'You do realize I'm going home.'

'I didn't mean as far as that, silly. I just don't fancy going on by myself. I might not be so lucky a second time,' she said cheekily. 'I thought I'd catch the bus with you as far as Hereford then take another to Birmingham.'

'Your money is all right, isn't it?' He remembered she'd mentioned a budget. They'd shared expenses at night.

'More or less.'

'Then, of course you must go home.' He would have liked to offer to lend her something – but she was fiercely independent and he didn't want to offend her.

Waiting for the Birmingham bus, he said idly:

'I did enjoy that walk. Wouldn't mind doing it again sometime. Do you walk often?'

'Mal and I went walking once a fortnight. Usually on our own. I suppose I'll have to find someone else to go with in future.'

'You could always join a club.'

She made a face. 'Not my scene.'

It wasn't his scene, either, but he thought a rambling-club was a lot safer for a young woman than walking unaccompanied. Then he had a suspicion that she was completely amoral, like all the younger generation. Catching himself in the act of typifying the generation gap, Joe kicked himself mentally. There wasn't much of a difference in their ages, after all, for all she was nearer his daughter's age than his.

'What I mean is, I really would like to do it again, with you.' He was floundering, like any callow youth.

Tessa grinned. 'I thought you didn't go in for double beds.'

'I didn't mean that,' he insisted, catching hold of her hand. She did not pull away, so he took heart. 'It's a long time since I enjoyed a walk so much.' It was the truth. Neither Amanda nor Sara had ever been keen walkers and, once their children had come, outings had assumed the spontaneity of a route march. They both enjoyed the countryside, but their idea of a day there usually entailed finding either a country carpark with picnic tables and scarcely moving more than 200 yards from the car, or some attraction that would divert the young.

'Look,' he said impulsively, 'suppose we meet at the bus station in Birmingham on Friday night in two weeks' time?'

He waited for divine judgement.

'Isn't your wife going to ask questions?'

'I'd already arranged to go and see my Aunt Ethel. I can still go, but before we meet.' Inwardly he groaned. Aunt Ethel, again? But he couldn't say: *My wife doesn't understand me.* Tessa would probably laugh. 'We could make Ludlow our centre,' he continued eagerly, persuasively naming a good hotel. 'I'll book us a room. Make it six o'clock? Then we'd be in time for dinner. Of course, if you're not there, I'll know you have something better to do. No explanations needed.' Not only was he incapable of walking away without compromising himself further, he was even selling himself short now, he thought in disgust.

'If you like.'

It was agreement, if hardly enthusiastic. The bus driver was preparing to move out. As Tessa put her foot on the bottom step Joe caught hold of her, kissing her lips clumsily. And then she had gone.

Once more companionless, Joe began dispassionately to review his behaviour since he had left home. Whatever had possessed him to make such a stupid suggestion? It was not his style, for he never did things without weighing the consequences. And now the last thing he needed was a further complication of this sort. That kiss at the end. Tessa probably thought she'd been propositioned. This very moment she was most likely laughing at his inept attempt at seduction before she expunged his face from her memory. Well, there was no need for him to turn up in Birmingham, after all. And if he didn't, he hardly thought she'd come looking for him. She'd soon find a younger man more to her taste.

Back at Ty Mawr, Joe was plunged into a drama of blocked drains.

'The things you women allow to go down sinks,' he grumbled, lying on his back, stripped to singlet and old jeans, his right arm through a hole in the wall and down into a main drain up as far as his armpit, cold greasy water lapping his flesh.

'Don't exaggerate, Joe,' Sara said wearily. 'Why is it this sort of thing always happens when there's no plumber available?' She had spent the greater part of the day in the chicken-run. A flooded kitchen floor was the last thing she needed.

'Erg! Got it!' Joe exclaimed, as he retrieved a ball of indeterminate matter. 'Hand me that hosepipe now and let's see if the water'll run through. Turn the tap on slowly. Slowly!' he yelled, as he got drenched.

The crisis of mopping up over, Harriet sent her mother to sit down with a gin and tonic.

'I'll get supper,' she said firmly. 'You go and talk to Dad.'

Joe was then, belatedly, welcomed home properly, with hugs and a drink and a hasty did-you-have-a-good-time-dear? To which question no one stopped for an answer, being more concerned with telling him what had occurred while he was away. Only natural, he considered patronizingly, to want to share their little doings with him.

'You've caught the sun, Dad,' Harriet remarked.

'The fresh air and exercise seem to have done you good, Joe,' Amanda said at supper. 'You sound a lot brighter, too.'

'I do feel fitter,' Joe agreed expansively.

'You'll have to do it again, Dad.'

'Yes, why not?' That was Sara, restored to good humour now the crisis was over.

Joe appeared to consider the matter.

'Not as a regular thing. Well, not every week. But occasionally. Go on a Saturday, come home on Sunday. Perhaps take one of you with me?' he suggested daringly.

'Not me,' Harriet answered promptly. 'Thanks all the same.'

'If you really want company—' began Amanda.

'It's not that I was lonely,' Joe assured her at once. 'I just thought someone else might like a change.'

'I was only going to suggest you joined the Ramblers, or something,' Amanda said. 'I don't think I could possibly spare the time. Not at present. I've too much reading to do.'

'I could do that. Not sure I wouldn't rather be independent,' Joe said. 'I met up with a group one night . . .' And for the rest of the meal he regaled them with carefully edited snippets which had the desired effect of boring the family so much that everyone carefully avoided any return to the subject on subsequent evenings.

He would not go, he decided. It had been a brief encounter, no more. If he went looking for a relationship – for inevitably that would be the outcome, it would be a disaster.

'Do you have to be away this weekend?' Sara asked, coming into Joe's room while he was packing. Nicola was sitting on the window seat, watching him. 'The goats are arriving and I need to make sure the fencing is absolutely secure.'

'Do they really have to be kept in a field?' Nicola protested.

'You surely don't intend goats to roam free, do you?' Joe said in alarm. 'Aren't they supposed to eat everything in sight?'

'I guess once they're used to us we can just tether them, but not at first. Anyway, I could do with your help after all.'

'I'll help, Mum,' Harriet, passing the door and overhearing the conversation, offered. 'I've been looking forward to the goats.'

'Me, too,' said Nicola. 'Will you teach me to milk them?'

'I think I may have to learn the technique myself first.' Sara laughed, hugging her small daughter. 'Anyway, thanks, love.' She smiled at Harriet. 'That'd be great.' Sara and Harriet were getting on better than they had before. Harriet had a waitressing job for the summer but as it only involved the evenings she often helped out. 'Though I suppose this would be the best weekend for you to go walking, Joe, with John and Fay coming the weekend after.' They did not see the two very often nowadays, which disappointed Amanda, but Fay had become strait-laced about Ty Mawr and its inhabitants and had to be persuaded to visit at all.

'Right, then.' Joe beamed at them all. 'Of course, if it rains I'll probably leave it anyway.' Hedging his bets? Just in case Tessa didn't turn up?

'And you'll see Aunt Ethel, too?' asked Amanda.

'Oh, yes. We've made our peace all right. I could even stay the night with her, if the weather turns.' He'd have to go. It would be mean-spirited to allow Tessa to wait at a bus station alone. He'd not like to think of Harriet waiting around at a place like that. He did not like to think of Harriet having anything like the arrangement he'd got with Tessa, though after last summer he knew his daughter was no longer quite as innocent as he'd believed her to be. Tessa was no innocent, either. Most likely she'd lost her virginity at the same age as his daughter, but that did not absolve him from some sort of responsibility towards her. If Tessa turned up, they'd take it from there.

Tessa arrived, breathless, half-an-hour late.

'The bloody bus got caught in traffic,' she said. 'I thought you'd've gone by now.'

Implying that she wouldn't have waited. All the same, Joe felt a great sense of triumph. She had come. She was young, attractive, and wanted to be with him.

'You're gorgeous,' he said. 'Am I the lucky man!'

'To be going walking with me?' she asked demurely, sitting beside him in the car, her hands folded in her lap.

'You know what I mean,' he declared happily. 'I can hardly wait.'

'No, I can feel that,' she said, and her right hand fluttered unexpectedly over his crotch which to his horror began bulging uncomfortably.

'Tessa! What are you doing?' he yelped. 'Look at the traffic. Do you want me to have an accident?' He squealed to a sudden halt at a set of traffic lights which had turned red.

Tessa smiled sweetly and removed her hand, making an impolite gesture to a lorry driver with a height advantage.

'Up to you,' she shrugged, and giggled.

Joe gulped and, grinding the gears, he looked frantically for the signs for Ludlow.

By Sunday afternoon, Joe was enraptured by the girl. They had walked all day Saturday but healthy tiredness – and a splendid dinner – sent them to bed early. Too early for sleep. As he dropped her off at the bus station Joe wished fervently that he did not have to wait for another fortnight before seeing her again.

He exhibited, over the next few weeks, classic symptoms of advanced infatuation: sweating palms while he waited for her at the bus station (he always arrived far too early, then regretted it), the lurch of the stomach when she came into view, jaunty step, head held high with her springy hair bouncing with life.

He was even able to dismiss the inevitable jarring of an abrasive personality as immaturity which his influence would cure. She thought he returned to an unloved and unloving wife. He was determined to conceal the truth at all costs. In case he lost her. Romantically yearning for her during the week, Joe made up conversations in which he told her the truth and persuaded her to join his family at Ty Mawr, that option being delightful, if totally unfeasible.

Only occasionally did he think: *This can't last.*

Chapter Eighteen

Amanda

The family at Ty Mawr realized that Joe was more often away at the weekends than he was with them at Harvest Festival when, after church (David having joined the choir), they all sat down to lunch. Even Simon was there, about to begin his second year at university.

'Why isn't Daddy here?' asked Nicola plaintively.

'I haven't seen him for yonks,' commented Harriet, helping herself to Sara's home-made redcurrant jelly. 'He's still in bed when I leave the house, and I'm in bed by the time he comes home. It's a pity about today.'

'It's a bit like when we were living at the other house,' said David.

'You'll have to forgive your father,' said Amanda automatically. 'He's gone to visit Aunt Ethel.'

'He's always going to see her.'

'She's an old woman. She needs his support.'

'Didn't you remind him that this is my last weekend at home?' asked Simon, with the arrogance of the student. 'I do think he might have made the effort to be here today and gone to see her another time.'

Amanda looked at Sara helplessly. She entirely agreed with

her son. But she never did criticize Joe in front of his children. Sara gave her an encouraging nod. 'Your father works very hard,' she interposed. 'Surely you don't begrudge him the weekends he's spent walking this summer?'

'I suppose not,' Simon admitted. 'Only he'd better be back early. I have to talk to him about insurance.'

'Let's forget about Dad,' Harriet interjected impatiently. 'I'm helping Dareth move a crate out of the potting-shed this afternoon and I need to borrow some gloves as mine have got holes in them.'

'You can borrow mine any time,' said Sara. 'Just so long as you put them back.' Mother and daughter smiled at each other. Their relationship, from the rocky time of the summer before, had cemented into something good.

Amanda was pleased to see it. But then, into her mind came the thought that while it was disturbing to hear Harriet dismiss her father, it did not seem to matter that Joe was not there. He had put very little effort into Ty Mawr since the middle of summer. His absences, disturbing though they were, no longer disrupted the routine that they had established.

'Do you think it's possible that Joe has found another woman?' Sara asked, echoing an uncomfortable thought that had occurred to Amanda on one or two occasions. The two women were alone while the children washed up after lunch.

'God knows,' Amanda replied. 'Though David is absolutely right. His absences are as regular as ever they were before we moved in together.'

'Except that we now share his remaining time.'

'Would you mind, if he had found another woman?'

'I don't know. What about you?'

'I haven't thought much about it,' lied Amanda. Then she flushed. Her relationship with Joe was not a thing over which it was right to prevaricate.

'Do we try and find out?'

'I don't think so.' Amanda shook her head.

'Perhaps not,' Sara agreed. 'Just yet.'

Amanda was not being strictly honest with Sara. She found herself welcoming Joe into her bed with less enthusiasm as the months passed. It was not that Amanda was unwilling. Increasingly she was beginning to feel distanced from Joe, as though he belonged to her past.

The moment came that evening, when she sat at her dressing-table preparing for bed and considered the matter objectively. It was inconceivable how much change had come about in little more than eighteen months: the discovery of Joe's treachery, buying Ty Mawr, the cancer scare, starting her course.

Amanda ran her hands over her breasts, smoothing the scar, which mercifully was the only reminder of that time. *I am a survivor.* She nodded at her reflection. *I may have been foolish in the past – and not just recently – but I am a survivor. I have so much to look forward to. Whatever happens in the future I shall survive that, too.*

But no one less than a superwoman could be expected to maintain her libido unaltered after all the traumas – and she was no more and no less than an ordinary woman, even if her lifestyle was a little other than the usual. She presumed that Joe felt the same, or else he would have made it quite plain what more he required from her. After all, the cancer scare was over, life had to go on. Instead it seemed to Amanda that Joe had evolved into her life's companion, her dear and loving friend.

So was Sara right? Did this mean he must have another woman? Reluctantly Amanda pondered the matter. She was beginning to think it must be so. Did she mind? Maybe sometimes, for they had been good together. Provided he remained her companion, probably she would learn to live with that (she would hardly be the first wife to have to accept a shift in her marriage). And then, new interests had come into her life. But as for Sara, she knew it was a different matter altogether. . . .

It was. Sara had confessed to Amanda that she loved the business of Ty Mawr, caring for it, nurturing the family, developing the garden.

'Did you know that I bitterly resented having to give up my little house?'

'So did I, though I never admitted it to Joe.'

'Nor I. Though I can't imagine why I thought that, now. After all, look at what we have.' She waved expressively towards the garden. 'All that out there, new friends in the village, my yoga class.'

'I know. We have emotional security and fulfilment, and there's the pleasure of watching the children grow into healthy young people.'

'If, two years before, anyone had suggested this state of affairs could have been the result of what Joe did to us, I would have laughed,' said Sara.

'I feel as though I've been liberated by, of all people, Joe himself. My life is enriched. If Joe doesn't feel quite that himself, who am I to criticize him for it?'

Amanda knew that Sara was aware that between herself and Joe the physical side was waning and that this state of affairs seemed mutually agreeable. She did have more than a shrewd suspicion that as a result Joe had found another woman. Did she mind? Did it matter? So long as the children did not come to believe themselves betrayed twice, no. So long as there was no more gossip, no local scandal. So long as Joe remained her loving husband, Amanda decided she could pretend ignorance. It was really all up to Joe.

Chapter Nineteen

Joe

It was too wet to walk. The rain had started as drizzle during Friday night and now the wind was getting up. The windscreen, already obscured by runnels of water, was now clogged with wet leaves falling from the trees under which they had parked. Down in the valley lights were being switched on and swirls of a slowly forming mist were rising from the little stream that meandered its way across the valley floor.

Joe shifted in his seat, his mind beginning to dwell longingly on a hot cup of tea, and a sinful buttered teacake. Surreptitiously he glanced at the clock on the dashboard. It was only mid-afternoon. He wound the window down a fraction to get some fresh air.

'Now I'm getting wet,' Tessa said crossly.

'Sorry,' he said automatically, and rewound the window.

Tessa sighed deeply. 'Joe, I'm in trouble. Not the usual sort,' she hastened to reassure him as he paled visibly. 'I've been made redundant. So I shall be even more hard up than now, sod it,' she complained. 'It's no good, Joe. I won't be able to go on seeing you. Maybe it's come at the right time. Maybe you were already thinking of ditching me?'

Up to that very moment it had seemed the only answer to what he suddenly recognized for what it was, a slowly declining interest in a relationship that had taken him over so intensely. Perversely Joe denied it vigorously. A bit too vigorously? An inner voice began to warn him to watch it, he was just possibly going to commit the indiscretion of all indiscretions. Another told him to live dangerously. Life wasn't over, by any means. Tessa wasn't over.

'Haven't I always taken care of you?' he demanded, turning to look at her, his gaze compelling. 'Why should you imagine things would change because of the lack of a bit of cash?'

'Oh, sure you have taken care of me,' she said. 'But it'll make a difference. Bound to, if I haven't any money to spare.'

'Suppose I found you a job nearer my home?'

'I'd take a job anywhere.'

'Suppose I found you a flat, until I found you a job? Somewhere like Monmouth or Abergavenny. Paid the rent for you? Things needn't change, then. Except we could be sure of seeing each other this winter. Actually, if you lived nearer we could see each other in a lot more comfort.' Joe gave an exaggerated shiver. 'Think of always meeting in the pouring rain, like this.'

'You offering to set me up?'

Idiot. Imbecile. She was safer in Birmingham. Did he have a death wish? 'That's what I'm suggesting,' Joe said firmly, over a pounding heart.

'All right. What have I got to lose.'

He saw her look at him assessingly, realized she was thinking that he wouldn't be able to, or he that he would change his mind. After all, most men decided against maintaining a mistress once they had weighed up the pros and cons, he knew that It made him all the more determined. That his decision had the result of Tessa's being disposed to be nicer to him than she had been recently, once they had gone back to their current B&B, only reinforced his certainty that he was doing the right thing.

Much later she asked him idly: 'Joe, do you have children?'

'Why do you ask?' he said, his mouth nuzzled into her neck.

'I just wondered. I mean, if you did set me up that close to home, would I be likely to bump into any of your family?'

'Even Monmouth isn't that small.' Still, he had himself been working out the odds. 'Most unlikely, I'd say.'

'So you don't have any children, then?'

'Er – my-um – wife had a baby eighteen months ago.'

'I see. That means you and she . . .'

'Well, of course.' He tried to make it sound the most natural thing in the world. 'I wouldn't deceive you into thinking I am about to leave my wife, you understand.'

'I see.' She sounded for once somehow chastened. 'How many children have you got, Joe?' she asked curiously, playing with the greying hairs on his chest.

'Um . . . Five, actually.'

'Goodness!' she sounded impressed, or was it appalled?

Joe saw that this was the time to reveal a part of the truth.

'Wives,' he said. 'Two of them.'

'I see,' she repeated.

She didn't see, of course, having jumped to the natural conclusion that he was divorced, Joe thought. Tessa was so transparent. He knew exactly what she was thinking: that a man might go through one divorce; he was hardly likely to go through two, maintenance being what it was likely to be. Not that he thought she had any inclination to want to change things, but at least now she knew where she stood.

'You find me a flat, Joe,' she told him, 'and I'll move into it.'

Joe held her naked body tightly while he stroked the hair from her face, new vistas of pleasure opening in front of him.

'As soon as I can,' he promised fervently. 'Tessa. You won't regret this.'

'No, Joe,' she replied sweetly, her lips close to his. 'I don't suppose I will.'

*

At home, where commonsense acted like a douche of cold water, the questions should he, shouldn't he? plagued Joe. There, he had everything he ever wanted. Tessa was a complication he hardly needed. When he was away from her he knew her to be a dangerous addiction. But, like an addiction, he had to have her.

He took a batch of tapes to his typist in the village. Mrs Evans, looking both troubled and defiant as she stood in her hallway, said, 'I've got this chance to visit my married daughter in Toronto, see, Mr Williams. Sent me the fare, they did, there's kind of them. The ticket arrived yesterday. So I won't be doing your typing until the spring, if it's all the same to you.'

His spirits lifted magically. This was providential.

'How splendid for you,' he beamed. 'I hope you don't find the Canadian winter too severe.'

'They keep their houses very warm, my daughter says. And I don't suppose I shall have to go out much, not with the baby being so young. Do you think you will find someone temporary to do the work, Mr Williams?' she went on cautiously. 'Only, I would like the job back.'

Of course. Then, she might change her mind, after a break. He said, not too eagerly:

'I know of a typist who became redundant recently. I might be able to persuade her to help out until you return.' That gave him three months. A lot could happen in three months. He thanked Mrs Evans profusely for all she had done, listened to her plans for her visit to Toronto over a cup of tea, admired for the umpteenth time the photos of her grandchild, and said goodbye until the spring. There was even a decent flat advertised in the *Monmouthshire Beacon* which came out that evening. Joe paid two months' rent in advance and promised that the new tenant would move in immediately the paperwork was completed.

Tessa was inclined to be critical.

'A part-time job's not much use to me,' she objected. 'What am I supposed to do for money? Though I suppose it's just as well there doesn't seem to be much to spend the money on in a dump like Monmouth.'

Sensibly, Joe kept his opinions to himself.

The flat was in a converted Georgian house on the outskirts of town. It was small, but light and well-heated. It was furnished to a reasonable standard and self-contained, with a small double bed in its little bedroom (or a large single, according to whether you were a pessimist or not). Joe toyed with the notion of a car. Perhaps later, he thought cautiously.

'You'll not lack for spending money,' he told Tessa expansively, by way of compensation. 'I promise you that.'

'You haven't even provided me with a computer yet,' she pointed out.

Nor he had. But that could be rectified. 'I'll bring over the office computer from home this afternoon.' He caught hold of her. 'I'm glad you've come, Tessa, I couldn't have borne it if I'd lost you. You'll see, we'll have a wonderful time.' There were other tenants in the house. Joe had already decided they would be no problem, for one of the flats was occupied by an unmarried couple and the third by a middle-aged woman.

He could see her relaxing, allowing herself to be mollified. As Joe began to kiss and fondle her, he felt her go pliant in his arms. But for once Joe's mind was not entirely on what he was doing. Now that he had Tessa where he wanted her, he could see that he was going to have to parcel out his time very carefully. The family at Ty Mawr had to be appeased for his absences this summer. Tessa herself had to understand she must share him. How to tell her this with-

out provoking an angry outburst had to be managed carefully. Angry outbursts from Tessa were what he least liked
about her.

He left it until he was leaving her, late the following
Sunday afternoon.

'I'll come in with an audio tape tomorrow teatime,' he said.
'I'll explain the way I like things done, then. You won't need to
worry about messages so long as you've switched on the
answering machine.'

She digested the information.

'I thought you wouldn't be here again until Friday, as
usual.'

'I reckon on popping in most days of the week, now you're
so close. As I did with Mrs Evans.'

'Did you, Joe?'

'Minx. Certainly not. She's almost due for her pension.'

'Days of the week, you said? What happens at the weekend?'

'I won't be here this weekend. There's a family do.' He
added the face-saving white lie. 'I daresay I'll be able to make
the occasional Sunday afternoon for tea.'

Tessa nodded, not taken in one bit.

'Tomorrow afternoon, then.'

'And you can do me a meal on Friday evening,' he told her.

'You expect me to cook for you, too? Will you be staying the
night?'

'Bed's a bit narrow for an entire night, don't you think?' he
replied jovially. 'I don't want you losing your beauty sleep.' Joe
was of an age to be a pessimist when it came to the comfort of
sleeping arrangements.

Tessa sighed. 'I reckon I'm getting very few privileges in
exchange for all this, Joe. Would you ever dare be seen eating
with me in public, for example?' She did not wait for the shake
of his head. 'If you want an old-fashioned mistress, Joe, that's

191

exactly what you'll get. Now, give me a kiss and leave me be.'

As he closed the door behind him Joe was more than a little taken aback. Old-fashioned mistresses cost, didn't they? He was beginning to wonder what on earth he had let himself in for.

Chapter Twenty

Sara

Looking back on that time when Amanda's cancer had been diagnosed, Sara could not believe how they had come through it.

After those weeks when she'd been in denial, Amanda was astonishing. It was as if she knew she was a survivor. Unlike Joe, who went to pieces. There were times when Sara found herself increasingly impatient with him to the point of taunting him that he was no more than another child, unable to see reality in front of him. Was that why it happened as it did, she wondered later, much later — that he needed respite from them all?

The loss of Amanda's hair was bad. Simon's hats were gold. On the days when a parcel arrived the tension eased. Sometimes there were tears, more often there was laughter, a sense that the world was not such a cruel place, after all. Even Joe's mood lightened and you could tell how proud he was of her bravery.

As for Sara herself, from the moment she found out about the cancer it was as though she was permanently touching wood. Was it callous, she asked herself, to be so thankful it was her body that was untainted?

Perhaps it was that which drove her to an extraordinary depth of care — though through it, because of that care, she came to have an affection for Amanda that grew as the healing process became established.

Thank God it wasn't me, whispered as she examined herself with rigorous regularity, became not a mantra but a desire to nurture the small things in her safe-keeping as well as the wounded one.

An antique dealer lived in the village. Sara had met him at the village shop when she was negotiating the sale of her surplus free-range eggs. Outside the shop they got into conversation about organic vegetables.

'So far I can only call them spray free,' she explained honestly.

He'd introduced himself as Philip Shawcross.

'I'd be happy to become a customer, when you want to sell,' he told her.

'I think I'm more likely to become a customer of yours, Philip. Ty Mawr needs several large pieces of furniture. Though I can't afford best antiques,' she added hastily.

'Tell me what you want and I'll see what I can do.'

Over the next few weeks Philip advised Sara on several local sales at which she acquired for a very modest sum two huge wardrobes (useless in small, modern houses), a battered pine kitchen table – which cost a little more, assorted pine chairs – which he assured her were worm-free, and an oak dresser for which she went over her limit and which he told her was an extortionate price.

'It's beautiful,' Sara enthused.

'No, it's not,' he said firmly. 'The top is a much later addition and the feet are modern. I'm also not too happy about one of the drawers.'

'Stop,' pleaded Sara. 'It's just the right size and the price was only a little more than I wanted to pay.'

Philip laughed. 'As long as you never accuse me of persuading you to buy this as a genuine antique.' He gestured quotation marks.

'Will you come to supper on Saturday? I should have the dresser in pride of place by then.' Philip was a widower and, she suspected, something of a recluse.

He looked uncomfortable. 'Will your – Joe – be there?'

Sara smiled, 'My husband. You don't have to consider my feelings, you know. Joe should be there, and you've not met Amanda, have you? You'd like her. Or is it something else? A moral issue?' She frowned. She did so hope Philip was not going to prove to be one of the 'brush-your-skirts-aside' brigade. There were a few in the village. It had not been altogether easy to fit in. If she ever would. An elderly woman behind the counter of the village shop had brazenly suggested it would take at least fifteen years, and laughed as though she actually meant it.

Philip seemed to come to a decision.

'I'd like that very much. But it's only fair to warn you that there are rumours about Joe.'

'That's only to be expected, isn't it.' Sara interrupted impatiently. 'We all know we live an unconventional lifestyle.' Philip said nothing. 'Well, come on, then. A specific rumour, or just general mutterings?'

'They say he has a girl in Monmouth.'

'Then if it's true, I'm sure we'll find out about it.' She was thinking: *I wonder if Amanda has heard?*

Amanda had not.

'I expect it's just gossip,' she said. 'I expect it's a bit of jealousy. You know. Old biddies with no sex life of their own.'

Sara giggled. 'I'd not thought of that. And Joe is being very attentive.' To her, he was, anyway. He came to her room several times a week, nowadays. Amanda didn't seem to mind. Not that he left her completely alone. Sara saw to that.

'Yes, he is. I expect everything is all right.'

Sara sighed with relief. More and more she was becoming sure there was another woman. Of course, if she really thought Amanda was being hurt by Joe, that would be different. Amanda had gone through so much and at last she seemed so confident, so happy with her studies. Simon had come home for a weekend before setting off on travels in Europe with friends. He'd brought one of them with him, a willowy blonde with a high-pitched giggle, whom the family bore stoically. Harriet was enjoying college, making friends and even had ideas about going into the market-garden business when she left. David and Nicola were both doing well at school and Miriam continued to thrive. Sara took all this in her stride, all the hassles of family life. She wanted no more changes for a long time.

On a cold morning in early March, Sara found herself next to Mrs Evans at the fish van in Monmouth's Friday market. As usual, there were several people queuing and they were all resigned to a chilly wait. The two women had only met twice before, though they had spoken over the phone in the early months of Mrs Evans's employment by Joe. Now, after exchanging the usual pleasantries about the diabolical wind that was sweeping through the square, Mrs Evans brought herself to say:

'I do hope Mr Williams is not too upset by my decision not to work for him again?'

'I didn't know you'd stopped,' said Sara, startled.

Mrs Evans explained. They talked about the joys of being a grandmother, the beauty of the Canadian scenery. How nice it was, all the same, to come home after a holiday.

'But I don't need the extra money, I've decided, see,' said Mrs Evans. 'My daughter said it was very silly at my age working myself into a state about new technology when she could easily send me a bit. I mean, I was very happy with my electronic typewriter. Oh, I know a computer has a lot of advantages, but you wouldn't credit the number of times I accidentally pressed the wrong key. I was so afraid I'd lose something important. I mean, you don't lose pieces of paper, do you? Not if they're filed properly.'

'Well, no,' said Sara, who had incurred Joe's wrath on several occasions in the early days of the office computer.

'A good girl, my daughter is, and always has been. She's quite right. I did work myself into a state. Something dreadful, sometimes. Well, I thought. There's no point. Then your husband said that the lady who'd taken over when I went to Canada was quite happy to carry on. That was a real relief, I can tell you. I didn't like to let him down. He was very generous when I went away, was Mr Williams. And you don't like to seem ungrateful, do you?' She paused. Seemed to expect a comment.

'No, indeed,' said Sara.

'I suppose it's his nature,' said Mrs Evans, 'being generous. My friend, Mrs Jones who serves on the WI stall, says he's been one of their best customers, has Mr Williams, since you've been living round here. Set up a standing order for a treacle tart recently as she only makes one or two at a time. And he does love his fruit-cake, doesn't he?'

'Yes, I suppose he does,' said Sara vaguely.

'Mind, it's funny he didn't mention her to you. That girl. I do hope he is comfortable with his arrangements.' Mrs Evans's eyes gleamed with the anticipation of the born gossip as she anticipated a gem of a morsel.

'I expect it was one of the times I wasn't listening,' Sara said. 'We knew Joe'd found a typist through the *Monmouthshire Beacon* and naturally assumed he was happy with the arrangement. I'd certainly not heard any complaints.' She avoided Mrs Evans's eyes, her gaze remaining studiously on the piece of salmon presented to her, the fishmonger's knife hovering midway. 'Just a little bigger,' she said to the stallholder. 'Yes, that's fine. I'll take it in the whole piece, thanks.' She turned back to the older woman. 'But thank you for asking.' She spoke graciously to her, having paid for the fish: 'I'll tell Joe you mentioned it.'

Like hell she would! she thought as she drove home, her shopping completed. Just wait until I tell Amanda, she thought, burning with impatience to pour out the whole conversation into a sympathetic ear.

Chapter Twenty-One

Amanda

'We may be quite sure Joe is satisfied with his arrangements, secretarial or otherwise.' Amanda responded to Sara's news grimly.

'So you do think it's true?' Sara was neither upset nor angry on her own account, she discovered, just furious with Joe for having been found out.

'That Joe is having it off with his secretary? It's obvious, isn't it? I suppose it started in the summer when he went walking. Combining her with Aunt Ethel. All that exercise!' A part of her wanted to giggle, though really it was scandalous. 'We were right to be suspicious. Then, the weekends stopped once the autumn set in. Abruptly, almost. I thought – whatever – had finished.'

'So did I. Besides, he was – is – still so active in bed.' Sara stopped, and flushed.

'Ah,' said Amanda. 'Well, middle age has sort of cast its shadow.' But she was smiling. 'Joe and I . . . That is . . . I thought we both felt the same way. And, to be truthful, the cancer scare and everything, well, I think I looked on you as – as a godsend.'

'The nerve of the man, setting her up so near,' Sara exclaimed wrathfully. 'I suppose he even calls in to see her on Fridays, after he's been to visit Aunt Ethel. And talking of suspicions, Mrs Evans said that Joe has a standing order for a treacle tart in the market. Now there's a thing. Amanda, have you ever actually seen Aunt Ethel?'

'Now you come to mention it, not since the party my parents gave after they'd come round to us living together. All those years ago. He said it was because she disapproved of me. Do you think . . . No. Not even Joe could be so devious.'

'Couldn't he? Something else we shall have to sort out, I suppose,' sighed Sara. 'Yet it isn't as though Joe doesn't make an effort,' she ended loyally.

'I'm beginning to wonder if we have ever known the real Joe.'

'Or are we just jumping to the wrong conclusion?'

'Oh, I'm sure Joe has another woman, and she's getting recompensed for it.' Amanda said drily.

'What are we going to do? I wish I didn't feel so betrayed, this time. I mean, I minded a great deal when I found out about you. What he had told me had been such a pack of lies. But I came to terms with it, eventually. Because of you. I began to see that what the three of us have is very precious. That is what is so galling, that Joe appears not to recognize just what we do have.'

'I'm not exactly jealous of the girl, either,' said Amanda. 'I suppose she must be very much younger. I am just so furious that he has put all this into jeopardy. After all our hard work, especially your backbreaking effort.' Amanda knew exactly what Sara had put into Ty Mawr. She touched her arm sympathetically. 'The thought that this place could fall apart for want of a bit of adult self-control. I could almost kill Joe, I really could,' she ended wrathfully.

'We all need Ty Mawr,' said Sara fervently. 'But you don't mean you would leave it, leave us?'

'I don't know. . . .' Amanda was thinking of her studies. There were so many other possibilities for work, new relationships – if she had the energy – even at her age. Then she thought about Ty Mawr. She so loved it here. 'That depends on Joe, I think.'

'So what we have to do is to find a way not to lose it,' said Sara bracingly.

Amanda smiled. 'Remember it was me who suggested our arrangement? Here's another fantasy. Suppose we found out where this girl lives. It shouldn't be so very difficult. Then, suppose we confront her . . .'

'Tell her to get out of Joe's life?'

'Maybe, give her an option. After all, I wouldn't want to break Joe's heart, if he really loves her.'

'An option? As in, go away or come and join us? You cannot be serious.'

'Perhaps she would agree to do all the paperwork here in return for bed and board?' suggested Amanda. She caught Sara's eye. After a moment they both dissolved into laughter. The mirth was genuine and brought with it relief. The scenario was quite absurd.

'That would cook Joe's goose for him.'

'And what if she said yes?'

The laughter was cut off abruptly as this possibility was realized.

'Why is it the women who have to make all the compromises?' remarked Sara ruefully. 'I bet Joe knew he was safe even before he began this affair.'

'To be fair to him,' countered Amanda, 'which may be more than he deserves, he could have left either of us at any time. But he never did. It was a pretty elaborate charade he set up, all those years ago. You have to admire his ingenuity. I think, maybe Joe can't help himself when it comes to women.' Amanda wondered why she had not recognized this before. 'He has to be nice to women. Recently I've been doing a lot of thinking.' Sara nodded. 'Yes, about the cancer, but also about Joe. Joe and us. That time when he first told me about Aunt Ethel. He admitted then he was scared of fatherhood. I believe it was more than that. I believe he had only then realized the responsibility of his encounter with adult sexuality.'

'Hey, that's a bit profound.'

'Joe discovered that relationships aren't just about pleasure, they're about responsibility too, in our case, to me and to his child. It proved too scary for him to take.'

'So where do I come in? Why did he add to his difficulties?'

'He wasn't doing that, at least not consciously. Joe was exchanging the heavy responsibility of us for the carefree pleasure of you.'

'But I became pregnant with Harriet,' Sara pointed out.

'Then when his sense of duty to you and Harriet became too overwhelming he was able to leave you for us. It was so easy.'

'Yet he seemed genuinely glad when I had David and Nicola. He loves Miriam,' said Sara, a defiant note in her voice.

'Of course he does. Credit Joe with some maturity. Though not too much,' Amanda added wryly. 'He's relied on us for so long to make everything all right for him, at first separately, then together, I suppose it was bound to happen that he would become bored, that he would stray eventually. Or contemplate straying. We don't actually know if this gossip is founded in fact.'

'Maybe we could find out a little more about this girl. Whether she's genuinely in love with Joe, or whether she is out for all she can get.'

'Mm. We'd have to be very careful, though. If Joe found out, he'd be furious. Do you think you would mind, if it turns out she really loves him?'

'Yes! Oh, I don't know. I daresay I'd learn to live with it. Perhaps it would be better if we do nothing.'

'Not quite,' answered Amanda.

Chapter Twenty-Two

Tessa

Christmas had come and gone – without Joe. In her warm, agreeably furnished flat which now contained many necessary additions: Sky+ TV, a DVD, microwave and dishwasher as well as the usual kitchen appliances, not to mention a drawer full of the sort of underwear she had only lusted after before and a wardrobe containing clothes that would do very nicely once she was back in the smoke, Tessa was relaxed and reasonably content.

She was, though, aware that Joe was restive. She thought it was possibly because with the coming of summer Mrs Evans would be wanting her job back. With no work to give her a wage – for she could not see Joe being keen on her taking a job in town – Monmouth would be unbearable. Tessa did so hope Joe's restlessness was not because he had heard any gossip about her for, as it happened, his fears would not be unfounded. A new interest had come into Tessa's life when one of the flats changed tenants. A young heating engineer called Matt took it over. His admiring glances became short conversations on the stairs as they passed and developed into exchanged cups of coffee when Tessa knew Joe was unlikely to call.

Matt knew about Joe, because Tessa told him quite bluntly that he was her lover as well as her employer. However, she agreed to accompany Matt to the cinema in Coleford whenever there was a film worth seeing. In fact, usually she drove him, for her Metro was newer than his Fiesta. Once, he cooked Sunday lunch for her. So far nothing physical had occurred between them. But the time might easily arrive when a change of allegiance would seem to her a very good alternative to what she had with an older man. Matt sometimes preened, assuming (erroneously) that in one department at least, Tessa was not very well off. For the moment, though, she considered that it was definitely in her best interests to continue her waiting game.

A week later, Mrs Evans called unexpectedly on Tessa.

'You mustn't think I'm angling for my job back, dear,' she said, casting a brightly curious eye round the sitting-room, quite openly assessing the value of its contents. 'I told Mr Williams I didn't want it, and I meant it. No. I'm happy enough doing the odd hour or so for an estate agent in town when he needs extra help, and I'm also busy knitting for my second grandchild.'

'Then why have you come here, Mrs Evans?' Tessa asked bluntly. She had not even offered the older woman a chair, let alone a cup of tea.

The omission set Mrs Evans against her. Not that she'd have said yes, as she was to tell Mrs Williams. But Miss could have offered. It had been quite a revelation, the wickedness of Mr Williams as related to her by Mrs Williams (in strictest confidence).

'My dictionary it is, see. I think Mr Williams took it by mistake when he collected the computer. I still miss it something dreadful when I come to do the crossword. And then I thought, well, I really should ask for it back. Ah . . .' in tones of triumph, 'there it is.' She pounced on the volume in question which was lying on a table by the window under a box of chocolates. 'It has my name inside the cover. E. Evans. Well, actually it belonged to my husband, but it comes to the same thing, doesn't it? Mrs Williams, Mrs *Sara* Williams,' Mrs Evans emphasized, 'suggested it wasn't necessary to bother Mr Williams but just come and ask for it myself. She knew I'd have to pass your gate to get home from the market. That's where I saw her. I do, quite regularly. Not that you can do more than pass the time of day when you're shopping, can you? Such a nice lady she is, isn't she? I don't really know Mrs *Amanda* Williams, you understand? I don't suppose I've had occasion to talk to her more than once or twice, over the phone, you know, what with her college studies and that. Funny set-up, isn't it? Still, you young ones nowadays understand more about that sort of thing than us old 'uns, don't you? I imagine you've met them both.'

'Both?' asked Tessa faintly.

'Both his wives,' replied Mrs Evans loudly, so that there could be no mistake. 'Well, both his women,' Mrs Evans sniffed, 'if you want to call a spade a spade. In my day you found a different sort of person in a place like Ty Mawr. Still, there it is. But, I tell you, my daughter was that shocked when I told her how it was. "Mum," she said, "I don't think you should be working for a man like that." Not that I'm condoning immorality, but times have changed, I said to her. For all your loose ways,' she eyed Tessa up and down in a manner which left that young woman no illusions as to how her relationship with Joe was regarded by one respectable member of the community, 'I daresay none of you means any harm.'

'Er – no,' agreed Tessa, her mind reeling with likely consequences, not the least her own precarious existence.

'My daughter was all for me giving up the job there and then. But I told her not to be so silly. Jobs don't grow on trees, I said. Then, the longer I was in Canada, the more I got to thinking about it. It is nice not to have to worry about my time, as I said to Mrs Williams in the market, salmon she was buying. I don't like it myself. I much prefer a thick piece of cod, don't you? I *certainly* wouldn't have left Mr Williams for any other reason. And I don't suppose you will, either. There's a really nice man he is, Mr Williams, and I always speak as I find. Still, I expect you understand his position exactly.'

Suddenly Tessa did, recalling things he'd said. Tight-lipped, she showed Mrs Evans and her dictionary out of the door. (Personally she preferred the spell-check – not that she bothered with it very much.) But for once Tessa did nothing hastily. She was housed, fed, clothed, and occupied by Joe. The nest egg his generosity was building was still very small (though the material benefits were coming along nicely). Leaving him now would be an empty gesture.

On Saturday night, Joe being occupied – family matters, he'd said – she went with Matt to the cinema. Afterwards, as they sat in his flat drinking white wine, he told her he was going away at the end of the month. He was being sent to Talgarth. Tessa allowed a look of dismay to flit across her face. This time, when he tried to kiss her goodnight, she did not turn her cheek but permitted herself to be kissed on the mouth.

She did not leave Matt's bed until mid-morning, and then only to make him some breakfast. A week later it was decided that Matt would not be leaving Monmouth alone.

Chapter Twenty-Three

Sara

Joe had a feverish cold. It had gone to his chest and the hacking cough, sleepless nights and general debility had totally drained his energy.

'He insists it's flu. Is it just Joe, or is it a male thing, this propensity to be a bad patient?' Amanda asked Sara, with some exasperation.

'Joe has always been one of the worst. At least, with me. He said the thought of coping with any work at the moment, as well as a sodden handkerchief, made him feel quite faint, but when I suggested I should ring the office to say he was indisposed he insisted on telephoning himself to say he'd not be in until the end of the week.'

'She sounded quite callous,' he had grumbled to Sara, supposedly of his secretary. 'Said that she had always been highly susceptible to germs and I wasn't to come near the works until I am quite cured.'

'I think we know why he spoke to her himself.'

'She's gone, you know,' said Sara. 'I went to the house yesterday and rang the bell. While I was waiting, one of the other tenants came out and told me Tessa had gone to Talgarth with her new man.'

'A new man? Ah. I suppose Joe is going to be a bit put out.'

'To say the very least.'

'Do you think we should . . . do anything?'

'Maybe just be there, when he needs us.'

So Joe surrendered to his family's ministrations, the soothing presence of Sara who fetched him paracetamol and lemon drinks. Eventually, though, the angels who had ministered to his misery told him bluntly that he was much better and could do with some fresh air.

'I'll see if there's anything for me to sign,then go for a short walk.'

Go and see what Tessa's been up to, thought Sara. After her conversation with Amanda, she decided to follow him and parked at a discreet distance while Joe let himself into the flat. He was there for quite some time. When he emerged he looked so shattered that Sara became really worried and instead of going home to do some digging in the garden, as she had planned, once more she followed him.

Joe took himself off for a walk in Staunton woods. There was a bitterly cold wind blowing and the sun shone only patchily. Sara found him sitting on the top of Far Harkening Rock and regarding the woods below him, their winter starkness blurred by a misty haze of tender green. Beside him there was already a hint of azure in the swelling blue of the bluebells and behind him a pair of blackbirds resumed the feverish feeding of their young.

He moved uneasily and Sara, from a few yards away, gave a little gasp and trod on a dead branch which snapped loudly under her weight. He turned.

'What are you doing here?' he exclaimed.

'I followed you.'

'I can see that. But why?'

'I wanted to make sure you were all right.'

He frowned at her. 'I haven't been that ill . . . Oh.'

There was a pause. Sara approached him slowly.

'Don't get me wrong. I wouldn't even think of jumping off after you. Or even peering over the edge.' She could see conflicting emotions crossing his face – guilt, chagrin, nonchalance. After a while he gave up.

'I guess you know about Tessa?'

'Yes, we do.'

'Did she go because of you?' he demanded then, angrily.

'No. That is . . . she found out about Ty Mawr. Our arrangements. She didn't have to go, Joe,' Sara insisted. 'Amanda and I—'

'How did you find out?'

Sara sighed. 'Gossip. You know what a small town is like. You can't hide anything for long.'

'Obviously not. It was stupid of me to be complacent. So. What were you going to say about Amanda?'

'We decided we could cope, if Tessa loved you enough to stay.'

'Did you, indeed.' He was really angry now. 'And what gave you the right to interfere in my affairs?'

'Don't be silly, Joe,' she snapped. 'What gave you the right to try to ruin Ty Mawr?'

'I tried very hard not to.'

'Not hard enough, considering you never had to get into this mess in the first place. How could you betray us in this way? Do you think I – we – can ever trust you again? Joe, do you realize what you've done?' There was a catch in her voice that was unmistakable.

Joe got off the rock carefully, mindful of the considerable drop. 'I suppose so. Maybe. . . . Does this mean you're leaving me?' he asked, coming to stand close to her.

Sara sighed. 'No, Joe. I don't think I am. But whether I ever forgive you for this is another matter.' They remained there, just looking at each other. After a while Sara asked:

'What happened when you got to the flat?'

'You know about that too? Of course you do.' He kicked at a clump of young bluebells, ground them into the leaf-mould almost savagely. 'Would you believe me if I told you that my first reaction, when I got into that empty flat, finding it stripped bare of her things, was one of relief?'

'Tell me about it,' she said encouragingly, thinking that this was a start, thinking that hurt pride, that Tessa should have left him for another man, must have been paramount, rather than deep affection.

'She's taken everything. Even the computer. Not to mention the car. I've a good mind to go to the police.'

'Would you really do that?'

'I guess commonsense prevails. Thank God I've got back-up files. And do I really want the whole sorry episode exposed?' He grimaced. 'That is, do I want it exposed outside the family.' A thought seemed to occur. He said anxiously, 'Have you told the children?'

'What do you take us for? Though we might have had to tell them, if Tessa had become a proper part of the family.'

'I don't think that was ever on the cards. She wouldn't have cared to be number three.'

'It's not really a laughing matter, Joe.'

'Sorry.'

It was not a word that came easily to Joe.

'And there's another thing. . . .' She told him about the treacle tart and Mrs Evans in the market.

Joe knew what was coming before she spoke. He had always known they would find out, but now that they had he felt almost resentful. He sighed, his mind working overtime.

'Oh dear,' he said. 'Aunt Ethel is going to be so disappointed that our little secret is out.' Sara raised an eyebrow. 'You see,' Joe went on glibly, 'she's not been able to do any baking for herself for years.'

'So how does she manage?'

'Meals-on-Wheels for three days a week, a neighbour for the weekend and she gets a meal from a local restaurant for the other two. She can do breakfast and suppers, soup and such. The neighbour also does her shopping. One of these days she'll probably want full-time nursing, but she's a long way from that, thank goodness. Anyway, she felt so badly about letting you down that I thought up the tiny deception. They do a great Bakewell tart at the WI. I've often thought we should try it.'

Sara shook her head. 'Don't try to sidetrack, Joe.' She had more than a suspicion she was being fobbed off. Again. But if myth she was, Aunt Ethel was solidly constructed indeed. She returned to present concerns. 'As for the other, I thought we had become friends. Loving friends, as well as lovers. How could a friend do this?' she asked, not attempting to hide her bitterness.

'Where did it all go wrong? How can I say. I think I began to feel excluded. You know, you and Amanda adjusted to Ty Mawr so easily. Far more easily than I did. Sometimes I felt as though I had no role at all.'

'That's ridiculous,' she said weakly.

'Is it? Well, it's no excuse. I understand that and I will try and make it up to you, truly. And of course we are friends. I hope we shall never be anything else.'

'Well, we shall have to see whether your repentance is good enough, won't we?' she said, her tone hard.

'And Amanda?'

'Amanda's taken it badly, Joe. I really don't know how you'll make it up to her.'

Chapter Twenty-Four

Amanda

She knew he would expect the door to be locked against him. It was not. That he feared she'd throw him out of her room. When Amanda did not, Joe seemed nonplussed.

'Sara told you, about Tessa going?' he asked casually.

'Yes. I gather she walked off with all the loot.'

'Mercenary little bitch.'

'Joe!'

'I know. I know. It's no more than I deserve.'

'Why did you do it, Joe? Oh, I think I could have understood a one-night stand. But a long-term relationship! Another long-term relationship. How many more have there been that I didn't know about?' She was sitting up in bed against the pillows. In the soft light she looked very lovely, strong, an utterly desirable woman.

'There weren't any more. I swear.'

She sighed. 'I wonder why I believe you?'

'Probably because it would have taken more energy than you know I've got to have casual affairs.'

She thought that was shrewd, but didn't say it. Instead:

'Weren't we enough for you?'

'I don't know,' he said hopelessly. 'She was there. It was all so exciting. Like it used to be.'

'Oh, Joe.' Amanda shook her head helplessly. 'The cancer scare. I knew you'd feel that way.'

'But that made no difference to my feelings for you,' he protested. 'I just wanted you to beat it. When eventually we knew you had, I can't tell you how glad I was. Am.'

She suppressed the thought that immediately came into her mind.

'But your feelings have changed. You find me boring.'

'Never that.'

'You find me undesirable.'

'Neither you nor Sara could ever be undesirable to me.'

'But things weren't the same. Joe, we can't be exciting all the time. Life isn't like that. There have to be dull days.'

'Do there?' he asked unexpectedly. 'Why do we have to submit to dreariness?'

'Because if we do otherwise, we run the risk of hurting those we love.'

'I do love you.'

'I know.' *Or I think I know*, she amended silently.

'Sara no longer trusts me.'

'Give her time. You forget just how much she has to lose if Ty Mawr falls apart.'

'I'd never let either of you suffer, materially.'

'You don't understand,' she cried. 'The material side is irrelevant.'

'How can money ever be irrelevant? It never has been.'

'That's unfair. I don't think I ever badgered you for material things. Did I, Joe?' And when he shook his head silently she went on: 'I know you congratulate yourself on providing for us generously—'

'I don't congratulate—' he protested.

'But it's the emotional security we have here that is the most important thing. Why is it we can't get you to see that?'

214

'Well,' he began, 'I realize you all get on together.'

'You see, you can't even accept how miraculous that is. Have you forgotten already that your son and daughter almost started a relationship that would have been disastrous if it hadn't been discovered by us in time? I can't imagine what it would have done to them otherwise. As it is, they accept each other as brother and sister, no harm done. That's one result of us coming to Ty Mawr. Simon is doing well at his studies, Harriet is almost ready to chose a career. David and Nicola are happy, too. Isn't all that more important than satisfying a sexual itch?'

'You know,' he said slowly, 'I knew you would be the one to rail at me. I feared you'd even decide to leave me. I thought Sara would be less affected.'

'So did I,' said Amanda unexpectedly. 'You do know she has—'

'Has what?' he asked sharply.

'Whom. There's a man in the village who admires her tremendously.'

'You talking about that antiques man. The one who came to dinner. I thought he was a bit – you know.'

'Actually I'm sure you're wrong there. After all, he's only recently been widowed.'

'Well, it did seem a bit odd, to me.'

'They're only friends,' Amanda protested. 'I don't even think she realizes he is keen on her. But Sara no longer has to take what you mete out, Joe. I think that's what's made the difference.'

'To her, but not to you?'

'Oh, that's not true,' she cried. 'I love you, and I always will. But if you continue to be unfaithful, to us, I don't have to take it any more than Sara does. My work has given me a whole new perspective on life.'

Independence, she was thinking. Financial independence

as well as the mental strength to live off her own resources, if that was what she wanted. 'I can do whatever I want,' she said boldly.

'Would you really have shared me with Tessa, if it had been done openly?' he asked softly.

Amanda appeared to think about it.

'Well . . . ?'

'Don't push your luck, Joe,' she warned him, equally softly, her eyes beginning to glitter.

'Do you want me to leave?'

Stupid question. She found she was yearning for him, and not only the comfort of him. But a mature woman's surrender wasn't quite the same thing as that of a young, untried girl.

'Not yet,' she said and, unhurriedly, her eyes fastened on his, she began to slide the sheet to one side and slowly raise a bare, shapely knee. 'Suppose you come and demonstrate that it'll be worth my while to let you stay.'

Chapter Twenty-Five

Epilogue: Joe on Joe

I was a fool, setting Tessa up quite so close to Ty Mawr. I can see that now. Hindsight is a marvellous thing, as they say. The wonder is not that something sent her off hurriedly but that we were not discovered a long time before, else the end of the affair might have been a lot more uncomfortable. Tessa herself could have blurted out the whole sequence of our relationship to the world before she went, if she'd had a mind to it. I'd not have put it past her. Though I am egotistical enough to think it says something for our relationship that she's gone so quietly, I always suspected there was more than a hint of malice in Tessa.

Confession time: she'd been good fun, had Tessa, on her better days, but the relief that she is no longer here suddenly proves stronger than either curiosity as to why she's gone, or the desire for revenge. So it appeared that Ty Mawr had survived a crisis. The experience shook me, chastened me. I like to think I became once more the model husband and father I had always considered myself to be.

It was a Friday in July of the following summer. I had taken the day off to go walking. It was a good trek up on that ridge in the Black Mountains from Gaer Fort to Bal Bach and that day it was so clear you could see for miles. I felt healthily tired and contented with my life. In fact during that uplifting day I had decided, not without regret, that the moment had come for Aunt Ethel, that embodiment of the genes of longevity, to die peacefully in her sleep. I'd lay her to rest and start the remainder of my life with a clear conscience.

I'd had a meal in one of my favourite pubs, whiling away an hour or so until I went home and I'd come to the bar to pay my bill. It was quiet except for two men playing dominoes and in a corner, alone, sat a woman I'd not noticed before. I eyed her through a mirror that was strategically placed behind the rows of bottles. She was young, but not too young, elegantly dressed in a well-cut beige-and-white linen frock. Not in the least flashy. Mid-thirties, I judged automatically. No ring, I noticed, without wondering why this might be important.

She seemed upset. Her fingers, when she put down her glass, shook slightly, and to hide it she put her hands in her lap. The pathetic attempt at hasty concealment touched me profoundly. I bent towards the barmaid and jerked my head back in the woman's direction.

'On her own, Elaine?'

'Now she is, Joe,' came the reply. I could see what Elaine was thinking, but what woman couldn't do with a shoulder to weep on, or a sympathetic ear, having got rid of what was probably a callous bastard?

I smiled as though I'd not noticed any reservations.

'Local, is she? I don't recognize her.'

Elaine shrugged. 'Usk way, maybe.'

'Been a quarrel?' I probed gently, keeping the look of concern on my own face.

'Half an hour ago,' she answered more helpfully.

'I thought as much. What's she drinking?' It was still early. I settled my bill and also paid for another pint for myself and a gin and tonic for the woman. Then I took the drinks over to the corner table and put them down carefully.

'You look as though you could do with this,' I said kindly as I sat down, not too close, opposite her, shielding her from Elaine's inquisitive glances.

She looked at me, startled out of her misery. She did not seem to mind that there were traces of tears on her cheeks but brushed them away with a delicate hand, defying me to make anything of them. I like that in a woman, a refusal to be anything other than what she is, and she was quite aware of what I was doing, a woman who knew that an approach under these circumstances meant that a man knew her situation for what it was.

'I swear that it is not that I am inclined to make the most of this for my own advantage. Men are not all the same.'

At that moment I still felt good: good from the walking, the steak, the beer, from this serendipitous challenge of an unknown female. The blood began singing in my veins.

'Tell me to go away and mind my own business, if you like,' I said. Sincerity was oozing from me. And it was genuine. I have never stayed where I'm not wanted. 'Only, I do know that sometimes it helps to talk things over, especially with a total stranger.'

She opened her mouth, about to send me smartly on my way. Then the miracle happened. She scrutinized me more closely, and changed her mind. She stared at her drink, the one I'd provided, sighed, and picked it up.

'You're married, of course,' she stated. Her voice was low and musical. She did not even sound particularly bitter.

'Oh . . .' I began the obligatory denial. Then I stopped. Hadn't I had enough of deception? It didn't work, in the long run. 'You know how it is,' I said ambiguously. Then it was as if the truth emerged of its own accord. I said: 'Yes, I am married. Very happily,' as if daring her to query it. 'The name's Joe, by the way. Should I get Elaine over there to do things properly and introduce us?'

She smiled at that. It was a watery smile, but it was a smile.

'There's really no need, is there? Bethan. That's mine.'

'Bethan. One of my favourites. I mean . . . I like it. I really do.' Inside, I cringed. Not a sophisticated approach. Then I thought, surprising myself, what approach? I was only trying to be kind, wasn't I? However, the approach or whatever, or the alcohol, or even just the contact, had made Bethan relax. Only slightly, but it was visible to a keen observer, which I pride myself on being.

Bethan sighed. 'That's what comes of having an affair with the husband of your best friend. You lose all sense of your own worth when it ends. Never mind that it has to end. You deprive yourself of what really matters, the consolation of talking things over with another woman. Did you ever have an affair?' she asked abruptly.

'Er . . . well, yes,' I admitted, choking over my beer.

'Just like all men,' she said bitterly.

'Um . . . I wouldn't say that,' I objected swiftly. I mean, I wasn't exactly proud of the affair with Tessa, but I'd have looked after her. Like I had with Sara, and Amanda before her.

'So she wasn't your wife's best friend?'

'Good lord, no.'

Bethan shot me a glance. 'Does that shock you? That he was the husband of my best friend?'

I leant across the table and patted her hand.

'Of course not. These things happen.' They did. I knew that only too well, even if it wasn't the best friend bit.

She seemed comforted by that remark.

'Most people condemn it.'

'I imagine your best friend does – would, if she knew.'

'She knows. Now.'

'Then, it would hurt, losing her. Almost as much as losing him.'

'That's sensitive.' *For a man*, hung between us. She picked up her glass again, drank from it. Then she said, 'That's exactly it. You deprive yourself of what really matters, confiding in an old friend who knows you. One on whom you've always relied. There aren't many friends like that. You don't realize how important they are, until you lose them.'

I found myself thinking of Amanda and Sara, of Sara's accusation that she thought we were friends as well as lovers. How I'd nearly lost my friends.

'I don't suppose I'll ever find another,' she said dolefully.

Without thinking, I said bracingly:

'Now, Bethan, I do know it's none of my business, and I promise I'll go away at once, if you want me to, but why don't you tell me exactly what happened tonight.'

'All right. I think I'd like that. But not here. Besides. . . .' She stopped. Seemed to consider. 'You see, I told him to go, and he went. We came in his car. I'm sort of stranded.' She told me where she lived. It was Usk way, as Elaine had told me. 'I was going to call for a taxi . . .'

'I'll take you home,' I offered. I said it casually, as a kindly meant gesture. The last thing I wanted to do was scare her off.

'Won't it take you out of your way?'

'Not at all.' Though not quite true.

It wasn't all that far in the other direction. She only spoke once, to tell me where to go. I stopped the engine at her front gate. The house was in a cul-de-sac. Quiet. The house and garden were in darkness. I doused my lights and got out of the car to open her door. I followed her up the path, watched while she put the key in the lock.

'So, Joe. Are you coming in to hear all about it, or have you changed your mind after all?' said Bethan, standing at the open door.

I had a momentary qualm. I'd gone to the local pub. Elaine knew me, what if she knew Sara? Had she already started gossiping? How soon would it be before word got around that Joe Williams had been seen driving off with an attractive woman who had just split up with a man?

The Joe Williams who'd been taken for a ride by a girl half his age whom he'd set up in a flat in Monmouth?

That Joe Williams. Guffaw.

What if Elaine gossiped? What was there to gossip about? He was just a man doing a good turn. Besides, the first rule for good bar staff is to listen and never gossip and, so far as I knew, Elaine was the best. Anyway, I could always give that pub a miss for a while.

What a blessing that Aunt Ethel was about to make another astounding recovery — though it did occur to me that she might have to lose a few years or very soon someone would be wondering when to buy the birthday card with 100 on it and would Aunt Ethel consider breaking the rule of a lifetime and allow the family to put on a party for her. We couldn't have any of that.

What was I thinking about? I'd come with Bethan to listen to her troubles. There was no way she was ready for another relationship, even if . . . no, of course not.

This was, I realized, one of life's definitive moments, when we see events clearly for the first time, when there is the possibility of redemption and we move on humbly, or when we understand that our characters have been tempered by our actions over many years and are now fatally flawed. Could I alter my ways any more than the leopard could change his spots? More to the point, did I want to?

Amanda had forgiven me, Sara was coming round, but it had been made subtly clear that I was no longer the mainstay of anyone's existence. Would they take me back if I transgressed again?

Are all men alike, or do I prove Bethan wrong?

She was still standing on the doorstep. Now she held out her hand.

'It's getting cold with the door open. Are you coming in to hear all about it, Joe,' she repeated, 'or have you changed your mind?'

There was a hint of defiance in the cool depth of her eyes and at the same time her expression was enigmatic, as if she understood all the conflicting emotions that were besetting me. I held her gaze for a long minute, then I smiled, took the proffered hand and stepped over her threshold.